D1235989

A LETHAL JOURNEY

Elizabeth Penney

Annie's®

AnniesFiction.com

A Lethal Journey

Library of Congress-in-Publication Data
A Lethal Journey / by Elizabeth Penney
p. cm.
I. Title
2016948554

AnniesFiction.com
(800) 282-6643
Secrets of the Quilt™
Series Creator: Shari Lohner
Series Editors: Shari Lohner, Janice Tate, and Ken Tate
Cover Illustrator: Jonathan Bouw

10 11 12 13 14 | Printed in China | 9 8 7 6 5 4 3 2 1

Cabot Falls, Vermont
Present Day

"Are you ready to see the final fabric swatch, ladies?" Sofia Parker knelt by the Italian Renaissance *cassone* and lifted the lid. Sofia and her friends, Julie Butler and Marla Dixon, were in Sofia's bedroom, where the priceless quilt she'd inherited from Elena Baresi, her Italian grandmother, was stored. Pieced together from fabrics passed down from Sofia's ancestors, the colorful blocks represented centuries of history in textile form.

"I can't wait." Julie moved closer to stand where she could see over Sofia's shoulder. "Each piece has been so different."

"And the story behind each one has been fascinating," Marla said. "My skills have been getting a real workout."

"As if that's a problem for you," Julie joked. Marla was head librarian at Cabot Falls Library, and research was her passion.

Sofia smiled at her friends' banter as she carefully pulled back the muslin protecting the precious heirloom. According to the diary that came with the quilt, swatch number twelve was in the right-hand bottom corner. When she got a good look at the piece, made of deep-pink silk embroidered with gold thread, she gasped.

"What is it?" Marla asked.

"It's stained," Sofia said. "How strange. The rest of the pieces are in excellent condition."

"Too bad," Marla said. "Otherwise the fabric is gorgeous."

Julie peered at the discoloration. "This looks like a water stain. See how it's darker brown at the edge?"

"I think you're right, Julie," Sofia said. "Let me check the diary and see if there are any clues as to what happened." She tucked the muslin back around the quilt and closed the trunk's lid, then went to her reading chair. The other two perched on the side of the bed while she picked up the leather-bound volume and turned to the correct page.

"'*Número dodici.*'" Sofia read. "Number twelve." She quickly scanned the entry, written in Italian, picking out the words she could understand. A more thorough translation would come later, with the help of a dictionary. Her pulse gave a leap when she grasped the story behind the stained silk. "Listen to this. That swatch is from a dress worn by Aria Greco, a *scrittore*—a writer—who traveled with her friend Daisy Griffin on the *Titanic*!"

Julie's green eyes lit up. "The *Titanic*! That's so tragically romantic."

"Do you suppose she was wearing that dress the night the ship sank?" Marla asked. "That would explain the stain."

"I bet she was." Sofia's mind raced, imagining Aria proudly wearing the dress for the evening, only to find herself scrambling to get off the sinking ocean liner in time.

Julie rubbed her hands together in glee. "We're going to have fun with this one. I just adore the clothes from that period. And everything about that ship intrigues me."

"At the time, it was the largest passenger ship ever built," Marla said. "The White Star Line had promoted it as unsinkable."

"That's sad," Sofia said. "So many people died that night." She closed the diary. "I can't wait to find out what happened to Aria, both on the ship and afterward."

"Maybe we can get started during our vacation," Julie said.

Sofia's family, including her sisters, Gina and Rosa, had rented a cottage on Lake Champlain for six weeks, with each family getting two weeks. Happily, it was right next door to Julie's family cottage, and she was going to be there with her husband and daughters during the two weeks Sofia's family had the place. Marla and her son were going to stay with Julie; her husband, Mark; and their twins, Ellie and Cindy.

"That's a great idea," Marla said. "I can run by the library and check out some books on the *Titanic*."

"I'd enjoy that," Sofia said. "But I don't want to interrupt your relaxation time with my project."

Julie snorted. "You mean *our* project. I can't imagine anything more interesting to do in between boating and barbecuing than learning about Aria Greco."

"That's true," Sofia said. "Jim will probably spend most of his time fishing anyway."

"So will Mark," Julie said.

"What's that about fishing?" Jim, Sofia's husband, appeared in the bedroom doorway. "And yes, I did pack the poles and tackle box."

"Good thing. I was worried." Sofia rolled her eyes. "How's the packing going?"

Jim crossed his arms and leaned against the doorway, the picture of smug satisfaction. "All done, ma'am. And guess what? There's still room for the kids and Fergus." Fergus was their Border collie.

"And for me, I hope." Sofia laughed.

"If not, you can ride with me and Marla," Julie said, picking up the joke. "We're going over tonight. The kids are coming with Mark tomorrow."

Sofia and Jim exchanged glances. "What do you think?" Sofia asked.

"I think you should go," Jim said. "It will be a nice opportunity for a Pinot Painters meeting." Jim straightened with a sigh. "I promised Matthew and Luke I'd play catch this afternoon, so I'd better get out there."

"Maybe you can wear them out so they'll sleep tonight," Sofia said. "They're pretty excited." In addition to their rambunctious younger sons, Sofia and Jim were parents to Wynter and their elder daughter, Vanessa.

"It's more likely they'll wear me out," Jim said. "See you at the lake, ladies." With a wave he was gone, his footsteps thudding down the stairs.

"If I'm going with you guys, I'd better hurry up and get ready." Sofia jumped up from her chair. "Jim has loaded the Suburban, but I've got to finish putting food together to get us through until we get to that little grocery store near the lake."

"How about I pick you up at four?" Julie said.

Sofia glanced at her bedside table. *Barely noon.* "I can do that." She gestured at the diary. "I don't want to take the diary out of the house, but I think I'll take photos of the pages about Aria. Then I can work on the translation at the cottage."

"Great idea," Marla said. "I'll run to the library now and get anything we have on the *Titanic.*"

Julie pulled her car keys out of her pocket. "It's a plan. See you at four."

As promised, Julie and Marla arrived at the Parker house at four on the dot. After hugging and kissing Jim and the kids good-bye, Sofia stowed her belongings in the back of Julie's SUV and they were off.

Sofia sat in the backseat, and as she gazed at the view of mountains and farms, she reflected that it was nice to be a passenger for a change. Most of the time she was transporting kids everywhere or barely taking a breath between errands, housework, and catering jobs. She gave a deep sigh, feeling her shoulders relax. "I'm on vacation. I'm actually on vacation."

Julie glanced in the rearview mirror and laughed. "Finally sinking in, huh?"

"Almost," Marla said, settling back in the front passenger seat. "Give me a day to unwind and stop thinking about work."

"It will be so relaxing at the lake," Julie promised. "You won't have to go anywhere unless you want to."

"That sounds wonderful," Sofia said. She savored the thought of two whole weeks lounging by the water, swimming, reading, and resting.

Julie merged onto the highway, and they buzzed up through the Green Mountains toward Burlington, the state capital and Vermont's most populous city. But before they reached the city proper, they exited the highway onto US Route 7, which skirted Lake Champlain, New England's largest body of water.

After several miles, they turned off the main road and took a curving road to the charming village of Corinna. White clapboard houses lined the narrow road, and Sofia saw an antique store, a small grocery and gas station, and a café. "I hope we make it back here," she said. "I love antiques, and that shop looks so quaint."

"I'm sure we will," Julie said. "It's not far from Corinna to the lake. In fact, we're almost there, but we could stop now and get a coffee."

"I'm fine," Sofia said.

Marla concurred, so they left the village behind and drove toward the lake, which could be glimpsed occasionally through the trees. Tiny lanes began to branch off each side of the road, and Julie took one, winding her way past cottages, camps, and cabins.

Julie's vacation home was at the end of a point shared by only a few others, including the one Sofia's family had rented. Sofia didn't have the key, so they stopped briefly in front of Windward, as it was called. A white clapboard cottage with a wraparound porch, it featured a covered balcony that protruded like the bow of a ship from the second story.

"Very cute," Marla said.

Sofia, who had only seen pictures, agreed. "I love it." She could see herself sitting on the balcony with a cup of coffee and a book.

Julie started the car moving again. "We're just down here." She pulled up next to a rambling yellow cottage, also with a wraparound porch. A wooden sign tacked to a tall pine tree read Sweet Breeze. "This place has been in my family since it was built. Thankfully we've been able to hold on to it." She halted the car and put it in park.

Marla opened her door. "And that's fortunate for us. It's wonderful."

They spent the next few minutes unpacking their belongings from the SUV. Marla had a room on the second floor with two beds, so Sofia decided to bunk in there with her for the night. After dropping her bags, she went downstairs to help Julie unload food in the kitchen.

"Let's do chicken on the grill tonight," Julie said, setting a plastic tub on the counter. "I marinated these breasts in my special sauce."

"Yum. I brought salad fixings from the farmer's market." Marla pulled lettuce, a cucumber, and gorgeous ripe tomatoes out of a cloth tote.

Sofia set her food offering on the counter. "I brought homemade double chocolate brownies. Of course, if you're determined to eat healthy—"

"Don't even say it!" Julie laughed. "I'm dying for chocolate."

"Me too," Marla said. "They'll be perfect with these." To gasps of pleasure, she unpacked a pint of strawberries.

"Let me start the grill and I'll give you a tour." Julie uncorked a bottle of white wine and poured three glasses.

They wandered around the grounds with their wine as Julie showed them the beach and an offshore dock for swimming, then took them by the boathouse, which held kayaks, a canoe, and a motorboat. In the backyard, a badminton net, a horseshoe pit, and a couple of hammocks rounded out the amenities.

"Mark ran up here last week to get things out of storage," Julie said, "and you guys are welcome to use anything you want. And there are probably more boats at your camp too."

"The kids will love this," Sofia said. Still sipping their wine, they strolled to a pine glade that glowed golden from the sun sinking behind the mountains on the other side of the lake. An onshore breeze tossed their hair, making ripples in the glittering water. The only sound was the splash of waves against the bank.

"It's so unbelievably quiet," Marla said.

As if to belie her words, a throaty car engine roared down the dirt road, moving too fast for the narrow, rutted lane.

Annoyance creased Julie's brow. "Who could that be?"

"One of the other renters maybe?" Sofia hoped not. All they needed was to have their peaceful vacation disturbed by noisy neighbors.

"They're coming down here," Julie said. She began to trot toward the cottage, followed by Sofia and Marla.

A rusty and battered blue sedan beelined down the drive and squealed to a halt beside Julie's SUV. The driver's door opened, and a lanky young man jumped out. Sofia noticed two things—he had wild, curly red hair and piercing green eyes.

Spotting the women, he gave a jaunty wave. "Hey, Sis. The prodigal returns."

Monte Carlo, Monaco
April 8, 1912

Even here, on the sparkling French Riviera, renowned for its famous beauties, American film actress Daisy Griffin drew all eyes. Her best friend, Aria Greco, watched with amusement as gentleman after gentleman turned to stare, tipping their hats and bowing as the two women strolled along the Avenue de Monte-Carlo. One stout fellow with an enormous nose and walrus mustache even clutched his chest and rolled his eyes, muttering, "*Mama mia.*"

"I think he must be an Italian count at the very least," Aria whispered. "Perhaps you can overlook his unfortunate countenance in favor of his Tuscan villa."

Daisy darted an elbow into Aria's side. "Poky cold-water flat in Rome, you mean, to be shared with his mother—and grandmother." She slid large blue eyes toward Aria. "Why do you tease so? You know my affections are already engaged."

How could Aria forget? Daisy had set her cap for millionaire Edward Thurston, heir to a railroad and banking fortune. Aria could see the attraction. In addition to the allure of his wealth, Edward was debonair and charming. His dark good looks were a perfect complement to Daisy's blond beauty, and they would make a stunning couple.

That being said, there was something about Edward that

made Aria's skin crawl. She had caught the cold, calculating look in his eyes when no one else was watching and the overly proprietary manner he displayed toward Daisy, as if she were just another possession. Both alarmed Aria.

Or are my reservations an excuse masking a more personal concern? she thought. If Daisy did marry and retire from acting, Aria would lose the plum position of writing scripts for her friend. She might be forced to return to Boston, to help her mother in the family dressmaking business. Not that there was anything wrong with dressmaking. It was just that Aria was all thumbs when it came to sewing. In fact, she found it to be sheer torture.

Daisy's steps quickened as they approached their lodging, the ornate Hotel de Paris, sprawled along the waterfront like an enormous stucco wedding cake. "Do you suppose we managed to get reservations?"

Aria followed more sedately. "I hope so, since you want them so badly."

Daisy pranced up the stone steps, her heels *tip-tapping*, then paused to allow the attendant to open the door for them. "Don't you want to sail on the *Titanic*?" she asked Aria. "It's the largest and most luxurious ship in the world." She turned her twinkling gaze to the doorman. "Wouldn't you like to travel to New York on the *Titanic*, Henri?"

Henri bowed. "Indeed, mam'selle. She is a very fine ship. Many of our guests will have the good fortune to enjoy her maiden voyage."

"And I hope I'm one of them." Daisy bestowed a dazzling smile on Henri as she entered the vast lobby. "I'm going to check my mail at the desk."

Aria trailed along behind, drinking in the beauty of white marble arches and carved moldings, which led the eye upward to a pale-blue rose window. Although they had been there for two weeks, the hotel's grace and elegance never failed to move her. Maybe she should write a scenario, a short script, set here . . . Words flooded her mind, and she fumbled in her pocket for the notebook and pencil she carried everywhere.

A piercing whistle broke her concentration, and she glanced up to see Daisy, standing by the wide staircase and waving, a huge grin on her face. Everyone else in the lobby turned to stare, but Daisy seemed unfazed by their attention, whether disapproving or admiring.

"I'm going up," Daisy called. "Are you coming?"

Her thoughts fled like mist dissolving in the morning sun. Aria tucked away her notebook, hoping her scribbles would be adequate when she returned to the story.

"Working on something?" Daisy asked as they began the climb upstairs. "I have never seen a writer as prolific as you. You find inspiration everywhere."

"That I do," Aria agreed. "This one features a young American fortune hunting in Monte Carlo. I'll work on it after I finish the Wild West story."

Daisy stopped short, her full lips parting in surprise. "You are wicked." Then she threw her head back and began to laugh.

That was one of Daisy's best traits, Aria reflected, the ability to laugh at her own foibles. Rare among beautiful actresses, especially those striving for the top of the competitive theatrical heap.

Daisy leaned close, butting her shoulder against Aria's. "I adore you, my dear. You keep my feet on the ground."

"And you allow me to keep my head in the clouds." Aria returned her friend's smile.

Upstairs, Aria unlocked the suite, allowing Daisy to enter first. "Did we get the reservations?"

Daisy threw the mail on a console table. "No. Worse luck. I

told the clerk to send word up straightaway when they arrive." She glided toward her bedroom, unpinning her hat as she went. "I'm going to take a long bath and a nap, so I will be well rested for dinner."

"I'll be out here, working." Aria gathered the letters and telegrams and began to sort them as she headed for the balcony doors. One of her duties was monitoring Daisy's commitments and business affairs, and she thought she might as well take care of things while savoring the ocean view.

Fear jolted when she spotted a familiar emblem on an envelope—the bold logo of the Pan-Francais Studio. Turning on her heel, she hurried to the bedroom.

"We have another letter from Pan-Francais."

Daisy scoffed as she stepped out of her petticoat, down to her chemise and drawers. "So what? There is nothing they can do."

Aria wasn't entirely convinced of that, but she'd supported Daisy when she broke her contract with the French studio for reasons she wouldn't discuss. All Aria knew was that the director, Pierre Lafitte, was involved.

"Throw it away." Daisy padded toward the adjoining bathroom. "I refuse to let that man ruin my day."

Leaving her friend to her bath and nap, Aria returned to the balcony. Besides the studio's letter, there was nothing else pressing, so she pulled out her notebook and spent a quiet hour writing. She didn't throw away the letter, however. Such reckless disregard in legal matters wasn't wise.

A knock on the door startled her, bringing her out of her imaginary world. Daisy's door was still shut, so Aria hurried to answer before the noise awakened her.

A bellman stood there, holding two enormous boxes. "Delivery for Mademoiselle Griffin." Daisy must have ordered dresses to add to her extensive wardrobe.

Aria pointed to a pale-blue brocade sofa. “Put them there. Thank you.” She found coins for a tip on top of a bureau. “Is there anything else?”

He shook his head as he pocketed the tip. “I’m sorry, mam’selle, but that is all they gave me to bring up.” With a small salute, he turned smartly and left.

No reservations on the *Titanic*. At this late date, it would be a miracle, since the ship would arrive and then depart from Cherbourg in two days. With all the publicity, the voyage was probably sold out.

She heard the rattle of a doorknob and saw Daisy’s bedroom door open. Daisy stood in the opening, yawning and stretching. “What did they bring up?”

Hoping to distract Daisy from thoughts of the *Titanic*, Aria bustled to the sofa. “Two new dresses. Shall I open the boxes?”

Daisy yawned again. “Sure. One of them is for you.”

Aria paused in the act of pulling off a cover, which was printed with the fashion house *Maison Lucile*. “For me? Lady Duff-Gordon’s dresses are enormously expensive.”

“I know.” Daisy moved to a nearby armchair. “But you deserve it.”

Aria’s pulse began to race as she opened the box. Thanks to her dressmaker mother and her father, who made fine leather shoes, she was quite well dressed. But she had neither the pocketbook nor the excuse to purchase high-fashion garments like Daisy did. The actress had an image to maintain. Aria was merely the writer in her shadow.

She pushed aside the tissue shrouding the dress, gasping when she saw the shine of deep-pink chiffon embroidered with gold. “It’s stunning. I can tell already.”

Daisy laughed. “Don’t be a goose. Take it out.”

With reverent hands, Aria pulled the dress from its nest and held it up. It featured the elbow-length sleeves, slightly high waist, and low, square neckline so popular that season.

"It will suit you perfectly," Daisy said. "The color flatters your dark hair and eyes."

"I can't thank you enough," Aria said. "I've never owned a designer gown before." Lady Duff-Gordon's fashions were the very height of chic, worn by the titled, very wealthy, and stars of screen, stage, and music hall.

"It should fit," Daisy said, "because I gave them one of your old dresses to go by. But if it does need alteration, we can take it to the London salon or wait until we're back in New York."

Aria carefully set her dress aside and turned to the other box. "Let's see yours."

Daisy's confection was equally marvelous, although very simple. The skirt was draped cream satin, set off by a black velvet bodice, bow, and sash. The upper bodice was also cream, as were the sleeves. Most interesting was the slit skirt almost hidden by the draped fabric.

"That's daring," Aria said. "Very elegant."

Daisy stroked the silk with a slim finger. "Isn't it? It strikes me as almost Grecian."

"Are you going to wear it tonight?" They always dressed for dinner at the hotel, and tonight, they were going to dine with Edward and his mother, Edith. Another strike against Edward, that he always traveled with his mother. Worse, she had a dour nature and vinegar tongue.

"No. I'm saving this dress for a special occasion." Daisy stood gracefully and stretched again. "Let's take a swim in the indoor pool. There's lots of time before dinner."

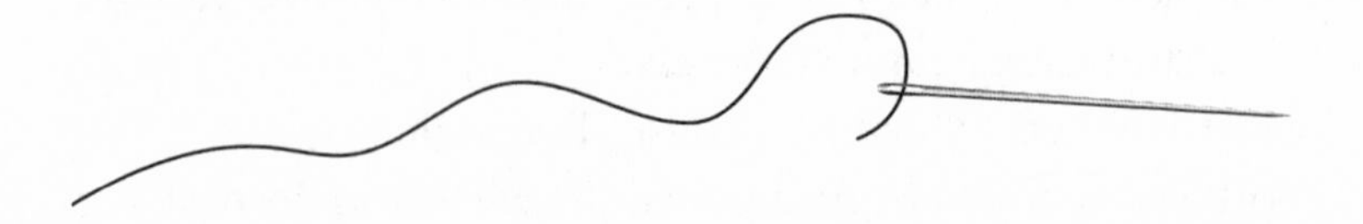

At the appointed hour, they made their way down to the lobby, where Edward and Edith awaited them. Edward's eyes lit up at the sight of Daisy, lovely in a pale-blue silk evening gown, trimmed with wide swaths of handmade lace. He strode across the carpet and bowed over her hand. "How are you tonight, my dear?" His eyes turned to Aria, and he nodded a greeting. She nodded back, hoping her true feelings were carefully hidden.

Daisy laughed as she extracted her hand. "I'm fine. How are you?" She swished forward to stand in front of Edith, who sat regal in an armchair, glittering diamonds adorning her neck, wrists, and fingers. One hand rested on an ivory-handled cane. "Good evening, Mrs. Thurston. It was a lovely day, wasn't it?"

Edith appeared to have sucked on a lemon. "Any day in Monte Carlo is lovely." Her eyes swept Daisy up and down. "Even if standards are . . . slipping."

A slight flush came to Daisy's cheeks, but she laughed off Edith's comment, pretending it was a jest. She took Edward's arm. "Let's go to dinner. I'm famished after my swim."

The couple led the way, and Edith and Aria followed, Edith obviously put out by Edward escorting Daisy rather than his mother, as was proper. *People often underestimate Daisy*, Aria reflected, *thanks to her sweet nature and candy-box prettiness.* But that pile of glossy blond hair hid a very sharp mind, capable of scheming and planning with the best of them. Nothing deterred Daisy Griffin from her goals. The fact that they were dining in Monte Carlo rather than living in a working-class Boston neighborhood was proof enough.

The dining room was about half full, the only sounds hushed conversation and the gentle strains of classical music from a string quartet in the corner. Aria loved this room too, with its ceiling painted with cherubs and clouds and the sheer amount of gilding and ornamentation encrusting the walls and ceiling. It was like walking into a Fabergé egg.

"Daisy!" A man with sandy hair and a thin face rose from a nearby table, one with room for eight but only occupied by the man and his dinner companion.

With a start, Aria recognized him. Henry Mason, Earl of Norwich, one of Daisy's former boyfriends. Aria had heard he'd married an American heiress. She regarded his wife curiously, noting a smooth oval face, sleek dark hair, almond-shaped brown eyes, and bee-stung lips. She was beautiful and, if that dagger gaze and the hand she put through her husband's arm as she stood were any indications, possessive.

"Henry. How nice to see you." Daisy turned to his wife. "You must be Lady Norwich."

"Please, call me Olive." The woman bared her teeth in a semblance of a smile.

It turned out Lord Henry knew the Thurstons—as family friends of Olive, they had attended the wedding—so at the couple's invitation, they joined them for dinner. Edith sat beside Henry, Edward beside Olive, and Daisy and Aria beside each other. Aria felt as though they were commoners flanked by British and American royalty.

After they ordered and the waiter poured the first glasses of wine, Edward turned to the lord. "How long are you staying in Monte Carlo, Henry?"

"Only one more night. This was just a brief stop after our tour of Italy. Tomorrow, we're taking the train to Cherbourg."

"We're sailing on the *Titanic*," Olive said. She turned fond eyes on her husband. "I was so thrilled when Henry booked our passage."

Edith clapped her hands. "Wonderful. So are we. We'll have plenty of time to catch up during the voyage."

"Not much time," Edward said, "if the boat is as fast as they claim."

"I don't care how fast it is," Olive said. "I'm looking forward to the first-class travel. It's as well-appointed as the finest luxury hotel, they say."

"I heard the food is first-rate also." Edith sat back to allow the waiter to place a bowl of soup in front of her. "There's even an exclusive restaurant modeled after the Ritz hotels. I will take all my meals there, I've decided."

Daisy groaned softly. "I'm just green with envy," she whispered to Aria.

Aria gave her a reassuring pat on the arm. Since being seated with the titled couple, neither Edward nor his mother had spared Daisy a word or glance. Like many Americans, they appeared to go weak in the knees in proximity of nobility.

Daisy's reprieve came during dinner. Their waiter approached and spoke to Daisy. "Mam'selle, there is an urgent telegram for you at the desk with a response requested. Shall I bring it here, to the table?"

"If no one minds, I'll go out to the desk and take care of it." Daisy's bright gaze traveled around the table. Hearing no objections, she put down her napkin and rose, followed by Henry and Edward. She bustled off and they sat again, resuming their discussion of a shooting party in Scotland. Olive and Edith had their heads together, quietly discussing people she didn't know, so Aria focused on her meal, letting her mind wander back to her Western story.

She was abruptly brought back to the room by Olive's strident tones. "Miss Greco? Are you with us?"

Aria gave a start. "I am sorry. I was woolgathering."

"I was asking about your association with Daisy. Are you her secretary?"

"No. I'm a screenwriter." At Olive's blank stare, she added, "I write the scenarios for Daisy's films."

Olive wrinkled her pretty little nose. "I didn't know that was an actual occupation."

"How else do you suppose the actors know what to do? They make it up as they go?" Edith's tart defense surprised Aria.

Olive flushed. "You're right. That was foolish of me."

"That's all right," Aria said. "Most of the gentlemen writers I meet can't believe I do it either."

"An actress like Daisy must have many male friends," Olive said. Her sly laugh seemed to imply there was something indecent about the way Daisy attracted men.

Aria regarded her coolly, seeking words that would reprove but not offend. "Yes, she does, most of them either titled or wealthy. Or both."

Olive's mouth dropped open, but before she could say anything, Daisy hurried up to the table, moving as fast as propriety and her narrow skirt would allow.

"Guess what, Aria?" She slid into her seat, fairly bouncing with excitement. "That was the White Star Line. We have reservations on the *Titanic*!"

"That's wonderful news, Daisy," Aria said. "I know you really wanted to go home on that ship."

Edith looked down her nose. "What class ticket did you manage to get at this late date?"

Daisy beamed as she picked up her fork. "First class, of course. And better yet, they gave me a suite." She shrugged delicate shoulders. "Apparently, they admire my work."

More like her beauty, Aria thought as she watched Olive's face turn sallow with repressed anger. She could almost sympathize with the new bride. After all, Henry hadn't merely been Daisy's beau; he had begged her to marry him. Several times, in fact.

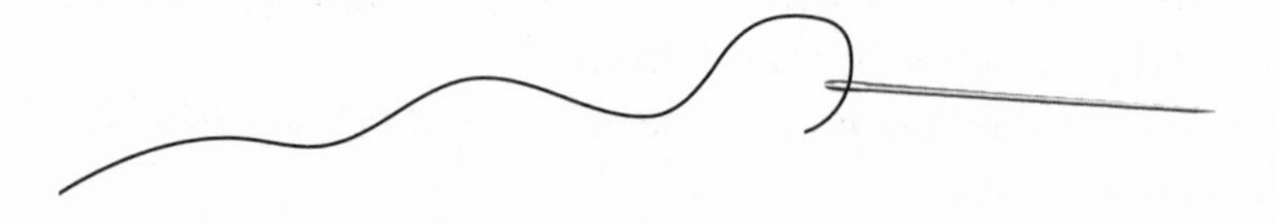

Monte Carlo, Monaco
April 9, 1912

"I wish you hadn't bought so many new dresses." Once again, Aria pulled everything out of the brass-bound trunk and piled it on the bed. "I'll never fit everything in there." Aria had a knack for packing, and once Daisy discovered that, it had fallen to her. She couldn't complain, though. Daisy footed the bill for just about everything, including their tickets on the *Titanic*.

Daisy regarded the heap of clothing with amusement. "You're right. I did go a little overboard." She snapped her fingers. "I know. I'll buy another trunk."

Aria regarded her friend with consternation. "Daisy, we don't have time to do more shopping. The train leaves in two hours." The first leg took them to Paris, and there, they had to change trains for Cherbourg. The ship was leaving port tomorrow evening.

"I'll ask the concierge to find me one." She shrugged. "I'm sure it won't be a problem."

Aria sighed. "You mean *I* will go ask him." She gave Daisy's pink silk negligee a pointed glance. "You're not even dressed yet."

Daisy gave her tinkling little giggle. "I am a sloth, aren't I? I shouldn't have gone to the casino with Edward last night."

"How did he do?" Aria asked, more out of politeness than true interest. While in Monte Carlo, Edward spent almost every evening playing baccarat or roulette, pastimes that bored her to tears. At least he had the money to lose, unlike some of the poor souls who gambled away their wages.

"He had a terrible night." A light glowed in Daisy's eyes. "But you should have seen Henry. He was a fiend at the baccarat table. He even split his winnings between Olive and me."

"She must have loved that." Glancing at the porcelain desk

clock, Aria moved toward the door. "I'd better get downstairs if they're to locate a trunk."

"Aria, do you think I . . ." Her voice sounded choked.

Aria stopped short. "Do I think you what?" Seeing the pained expression on her friend's face, she made a shrewd guess. "Do I think you made a mistake turning Henry down?"

Daisy put a hand to her throat. "How did you know what I was thinking?"

Aria crossed her arms and cocked her head. "Come on, Daisy. I know you better than anyone. Henry is a nice man, quite handsome too, so it's expected that you might second-guess your decision. But remember what you said when he proposed? There wasn't a spark between you. He was more a brother than a beau. Does that ring a bell?"

Daisy bit her lip. "Did I say all that? Then it must be true." Her glance fell on the clock, and she gave a little yelp. "You're right, it is late. I'd better wash up." She scurried for her bedroom, her nightgown flying out behind her.

As Aria headed for the concierge's desk where it was hoped they could have yet another miracle, she prayed that Daisy would drop her false regrets. All they needed while cloistered on a ship was for her to flirt with Henry and set off a firestorm of trouble. Daisy might have been lukewarm during their romance, but Henry had been certain she was the woman for him. Judging by the look in his eyes when he'd spotted Daisy, Aria sensed he still carried a torch. Had he married Olive for her fortune? Many of the nobility with huge and unprofitable estates were doing that these days.

Halfway down the stairs, a thought jolted her. *Maybe Daisy's doubts were about Edward, not her affections toward Henry.* Now that was a flame she wouldn't mind fanning.

Back upstairs, she found Daisy dressed and halfheartedly folding undergarments. "Any luck?" Daisy asked.

"Yes, they are sending someone out to an outfitter immediately. We should have a trunk within half an hour." Aria reached into her pocket. "There was a note for you."

Daisy picked up the pile of bloomers and dropped them into the trunk. "Go ahead and open it."

Aria broke the seal with her fingers, noticing there was nothing on the envelope but Daisy's name, written in block letters. She withdrew a single sheet, unfolded it, and scanned the words.

She almost dropped it in shock.

Be careful, the note read. *The truth will come out.*

Corinna, Vermont
Present Day

"Ian! What are you doing here?" Julie reached his side and gave him a big hug.

He hugged her back, a look of embarrassed pleasure on his face. "Whoa, don't strangle me." With a laugh, Ian disengaged.

Julie put her hands on her hips. "I haven't seen you for months. Where have you been?"

Ian ran a hand through his unruly hair. "Oh, here and there." His gaze went to Sofia and Marla. "Introduce me to your friends."

"I'm sorry. These are my friends from Cabot Falls." Julie threaded her arm through Ian's. "Sofia Parker, Marla Dixon, this is my little brother, Ian Marshall."

Sofia smiled at the sight of the much taller Ian beside his "big" sister. "Nice to meet you, Ian." Marla echoed her greeting.

"Sorry to barge in," Ian said, "but I was hoping to spend the night."

"Of course," Julie said. "There's plenty of room." She hit the side of her head. "Oh no. I forgot the charcoal. I hope it hasn't turned into ash."

"Let me take over." Ian winked at Sofia and Marla. "I'm the grilling king."

Julie steered her brother toward the grill near the back door, while Sofia and Marla went to the kitchen to carry the rest of the meal and table settings to the front screen porch, where there was a long table with room for twenty.

"I think we'll be having a lot of meals right here," Marla said. "This is perfect."

Picturing their combined families eating around the big table, Sofia had to agree. "Maybe we can take turns cooking."

Marla cocked her head toward the sounds of friendly argument coming from the grill. "If Ian's still around, he can alternate grilling with Jim and Mark."

"What is it about men and grills?" Sofia folded napkins and placed them on the place mats. "Jim will barely turn a knob on the stove, but show him a grill and he insists on taking over."

"The combination of meat and fire?" Marla shrugged. "Tim runs our grill, so they certainly start young." Marla's husband, Ryan, had died ten years before, and their fifteen-year-old son, Tim, regarded himself as the man of the house.

"Maybe he and Luke can cook for us one night," Sofia said. "I know Luke would enjoy that."

Sofia and Marla pulled together the meal with the exception of the grilled meat, passing the next quarter hour with small talk.

"Do you suppose Julie and Ian have forgotten about us?" Sofia asked. "I know it's been a while since they've seen each other, but maybe we need an excuse to go check on them."

"Great idea." Marla set down plates. "How about a pitcher of ice water?" She went to the kitchen, returning with Julie, who carried a platter of chicken breasts, and Ian. He carried a soda in one hand and his cell phone in the other.

After grace, they passed the food around, each person digging into the scrumptious meal.

"This is great, ladies," Ian said. He stabbed another piece of chicken and transferred it to his plate. "Everything is delicious."

"I'm glad I brought extra," Julie teased.

"I'm a growing boy." Ian smiled at his sister.

Julie scoffed. "Right, at thirty years old. Ian's the caboose," she told Sofia and Marla. "A surprise to Mom and Dad and us kids." She returned Ian's smile. "But a nice surprise."

He pointed his fork at her. "Good thing you said that." He laughed, then glanced down at his buzzing cell phone with a frown. "I don't want to take that right now."

"Do you live around here, Ian?" Marla asked.

"I have an apartment in Burlington. I work at a property management company up there that does all kinds of rentals, including seasonal."

"We used Lake Realty to rent our cottage," Sofia said.

"That's my company." He gestured at the shoreline. "We handle a lot of the cottages along here." A sly look came into his green eyes. "I have to warn you, though. Champy was recently spotted in this area of the lake."

Julie groaned. "Cut it out, Ian."

"Who or what is Champy?" Sofia asked.

Ian gave his sister an impish grin. "You've heard of the Loch Ness Monster? Champy is our Vermont version. He looks like a swimming sea serpent, so if you see a strange dinosaur head out there, tell the kids to get out of the water."

Marla took up the tale. "I've heard there were photos and videos that appeared authentic."

"That's right, there are." Ian gave a mock shudder. "Just when you thought it was safe . . . I haven't gone in deep water ever since I saw those online."

Sofia was skeptical. "How can that be? One prehistoric creature couldn't survive for thousands of years by itself. There would have to be a whole . . . herd of them out there. Or is it a school? Whatever you call a group of lake serpents."

"You're right, Sofia," Julie said. "Now, who wants dessert?"

"I do, I do." Ian's phone buzzed again, and he gave a huge sigh. "I'm sorry, but I guess I'd better take this. Please excuse me." He pushed back from the table and grabbed his phone, then went through the screen door and down the steps.

Once he was standing on the dock, out of earshot, Julie shook her head. "I love Ian, but he's always got some kind of drama going on in his life."

"He seems like a nice guy," Sofia said. "Good-looking too."

Julie smiled. "Girls are always chasing him, but he's so clueless, he doesn't even notice half the time." She stood and began to stack the empty plates. "Does anyone want coffee?"

"I'll take decaf." Sofia got up and began to help clear the table, as did Marla.

Ian returned to the table just as they sat down again to enjoy dessert. "Sorry about that," he said. "Work hassles." Sitting, he snatched a brownie from the plate. "Yum, moist," he said around a mouthful.

"Sofia made those," Julie said. "So it wasn't girl trouble?"

"Heck no. I don't have a girlfriend right now. But I do have a friend who works at the antique store in Corinna. Lea Jacobs. If you like that kind of stuff, you should go see her."

"That store did look intriguing when we drove by," Sofia said.

"I've been there a lot," Julie said. Her eyes brightened. "They specialize in maritime collectibles. I wonder if they have anything related to the *Titanic*."

Ian's brows rose. "The *Titanic*? They might. Why the sudden interest?"

Julie explained that they were researching Sofia's ancestor, who'd survived the sinking.

Ian's eyes widened. "That's cool. Otherwise you wouldn't be here, right?"

"Aria Greco wasn't a direct ancestor. I believe my great-grandmother was her sister."

Ian's phone pinged again, and he snatched it up with a groan. "Seriously, this is getting old," he muttered. To his sister, he said, "I'll take the bunk room, okay? And leave the dishes. I'm doing them."

"Thanks, Ian." Julie yawned and stretched. "I'm thinking about making it an early night. How about you two?"

"Yeah, I think I'll head to bed with a book," Sofia said. "Start reading up on the *Titanic*."

"I have plenty to choose from," Marla said. "I'll take them up to the room."

After her bedtime rituals, Sofia settled in one of the twin beds with a sigh of satisfaction. The windows facing the lake were open to the fresh night air, and she could hear the faint sound of water lapping the shore.

"This is nice, isn't it?" Marla padded into the room, dressed in T-shirt and boxers. She slid into the other bed. "I have a feeling I'm going to sleep really well here."

"Me too. Thanks for bringing the books." Sofia chose the top one, a thick tome that promised an overview of *Titanic*'s history through the sinking. Although she knew the basic story and had seen movies about the event, she wanted to have the full picture.

Marla fell asleep, but Sofia read on, marveling at the beauty of the ship and the well-known people who experienced its ill-fated voyage. American millionaires John Jacob Astor IV and Benjamin Guggenheim. Macy's owner Isidor Straus. Avant garde dress designer Lady Duff-Gordon. Film actress Daisy Griffin.

Sofia's pulse sped up. Aria's friend had been a film actress. Maybe some movies she had acted in were still available. They must have been silent films and among the first made. *I need to take a look online tomorrow morning.*

The next section listed the survivors and their destinations after the sinking. While Aria and Daisy weren't listed, a child named Etta Bannister had survived, and had gone to live in Sandwich, Vermont. She remembered seeing that town name on a road sign on Route 7. Etta couldn't possibly still be alive. But maybe she had descendants in the area.

Feeling satisfied by the results of her research, Sofia set the book aside and switched off the bedside lamp. *Time to get some rest.*

Her sweet slumber was interrupted early the next morning by shouting. Her eyes popped open, and she listened for a minute. Determining it was coming from outside, she ran to the window and peered out. Julie was out on the dock, pacing back and forth, calling out, "Ian! Ian, where are you?"

"What's going on?" Marla's voice was groggy.

"Something to do with Ian. I'm going down." Without bothering to dress or put on shoes, Sofia raced downstairs into the pink, fresh dawn.

Julie collapsed to the dock, sitting with legs crossed, hands over her face, rocking back and forth, keening.

Alarm spurred Sofia's feet, and she flew across the dewy grass and onto the dock. "What is it, Julie?" Sofia sank down beside her friend, putting a hand on her shoulder, hoping to calm her.

Julie turned a tearstained face toward her. "It's Ian." She gestured at a neat pile of folded clothes and a pair of shoes sitting on the planks nearby. "He's gone."

Monte Carlo, Monaco
April 9, 1912

Aria held the letter out to Daisy with quivering fingers. "Daisy. You need to see this."

Daisy dropped the pile of undergarments she held and took the sheet of paper. Then, to Aria's surprise, she threw it aside. "Bah. If someone wants to scare me, they should be brave enough to sign their name."

"But . . . but what does it mean when it says the truth will come out? What *truth* is it talking about?"

Daisy shrugged one slim shoulder. "I haven't a clue. The person who wrote it is clearly deranged." She turned to a pile of petticoats, seemingly absorbed in the chore of packing. "Why don't we put all the evening wear in the new trunk? That way I'll know where to find things on the ship."

Aria studied her friend. The problem with actresses was, well, they knew how to act. Daisy's appearance of unconcern was very convincing, but Aria found it hard to believe that the nasty note hadn't rattled her just a bit. With a shrug of her own, she decided to let the matter drop. But she picked up the letter and tucked it back into its envelope. Like the letter from the French studio, such correspondence was best kept rather than thrown away.

The new trunk soon arrived, and after frantic packing, they left the hotel and, with only minutes to spare, were dropped off at the railway station. The Paris train was already at the platform, huffing and puffing as gusts of steam escaped. Passengers and porters crowded the area, along with piles of luggage and freight.

"First class," Aria told one of the porters. He showed them to a private compartment, then took most of their baggage to a freight car. They kept only a few things: the clothing, toiletries, and amusements they needed for the six-hundred-mile journey, which would last almost twenty-four hours.

"I must face forward," Daisy said, as she always did when they traveled by rail. She removed her hat and the fur-trimmed jacket of her dove-gray traveling suit, then sat down with a sigh. She closed her eyes. "I'm weary already. Traveling tires me so."

After stowing their satchels and removing her own hat and the jacket of her hunter-green suit, Aria took the opposite seat, not caring if her view showed her where they had been rather than where they were going. Through the glass to the corridor, she watched other passengers come and go as they settled into their compartments. Edward and Edith were somewhere in first class on this train, as were Lord Henry and Olive. Daisy and Aria had already made arrangements to meet them all for dinner in the dining car.

The engine gave a few long blasts of the whistle, and as the chugging noise intensified, the carriage lurched forward. They were under way. Chills ran up Aria's spine. No matter how often or how far she journeyed, she always felt a thrill when setting off.

Aria watched the countryside for a while, enjoying the glimpses of greening vineyards and neat farmhouses drowsing under the midday sun. While she had enjoyed the glamorous bustle of Monte Carlo, Aria had an affinity for the tranquil beauty of rural life. Perhaps someday she could rent one of those stone cottages and write, her only companions a cat and bumblebees buzzing around a lush flower garden.

When Daisy gave a gentle snore, Aria laughed inwardly. She might as well venture to the dining car for some writing time over coffee and let Daisy nap in peace. To prevent prying eyes from staring at her friend, she lowered the shades over the corridor windows. Then she gathered her notebook and pencil before letting herself out quietly.

Many of the people in the compartments she passed were also dozing, lulled by the train's gentle rocking motion. The dining car was fairly deserted, so she chose a table in the corner by a window. The waiter brought coffee and cream, and she began to write, pausing once in a while to sip the hot beverage and stare out the window.

"*Bonjour,* Mademoiselle Greco."

Startled, Aria turned to see the French director Pierre Lafitte standing beside her table. Her cup rattled as she set it back in the saucer. "Monsieur Lafitte. I didn't know you were on this train."

In fact, she had thought him miles away in Paris, where she had last seen him, during the dreadful scene when Daisy had left his film set. Her stomach clenched in dread. What could he want with her?

He put his hand on the back of the chair opposite. "I had business in Nice and then spent a couple of days in Monte Carlo."

Sending unpleasant notes to Daisy in between trips to the casino? Seeing that he obviously wanted to talk, politeness dictated her invitation. "Would you like to join me?"

A grin creased his wide face, his thick mustache rising as he lifted his coattails and sat, shifting his body into position. Everything about the man was ponderous, his slow-moving body, his movements, his manner of speaking.

He picked up each piece of silverware, one after the other, and set them back on the linen cloth. "How is the lovely Mademoiselle Griffin?"

Better than before the threatening letter from the studio. "She is well. Thank you for asking. Very happy that we're sailing on the *Titanic*."

"Ah, the *Titanic*. I am also sailing on her."

Aria took another sip of coffee, hoping her dismay didn't show on her face. Even though the ship was huge, it would still be difficult to avoid the director on board. He would likely eat in the same dining room and frequent the same lounges.

The waiter came by, and Pierre also ordered coffee. Once it arrived, he made a show of adding cream and several lumps of sugar and stirring thoroughly. He nodded toward her notebook. "How is the writing?"

"Going well, thank you." Aria drained her cup. Maybe she could make her excuses and escape. She shifted backward in her chair, preparing to rise. "I'm sorry—"

"I have a proposal for you, mademoiselle."

She sat back into her seat. "I'm not sure I should listen to this." She waved her hand. "Considering the circumstances."

The smirk playing about his lips revealed that he knew full well what she meant. He leaned forward and lowered his voice to a confidential whisper. "It is to your benefit to listen." He paused, pointing one fat forefinger. "How would you like to become chief writer for Pan-Francais? Or one of the chief writers, at least?"

Aria's pulse leaped. Pan-Francais was one of the largest film studios in the world. Not only did they put out dozens of titles each year, but they also were expanding into the United States. "That does sound interesting. But you know I am committed to Daisy Griffin right now, and as long as I am, I cannot work for you." However, if Daisy did get married, leaving her to fend for herself . . .

"Ah. That is what I wish to discuss. Perhaps such a good friend as yourself"—again the smirk—"might be able to convince the mademoiselle that fulfilling her contract would be a wise course of action."

So that was his ploy. He didn't want to hire her because of her skill but rather her ability to wrangle Daisy back into the contract. Aria stood abruptly, sending her chair backward. "I'm sorry, monsieur. I cannot, and will not, coerce Daisy into an untenable situation to benefit myself."

"Think about it, mademoiselle. That is all I ask."

Without answering, Aria swept from the dining car, painfully aware of the stares of the few people in the car. Stares that followed her abrupt departure. Feeling her chin tremble, she forced a smile to her lips. Otherwise, she would burst into tears of rage and disappointment. How cruel to manipulate her that way, using her desire for a career as bait. Pierre Lafitte was a devil.

Aria didn't mention Pierre's offer to Daisy or even that he was on the train, hoping that by a miracle, she wouldn't see him. There was only one close call, during dinner when he took a table at the other end of the dining car. But Daisy, busy chatting with Henry and Edward, didn't spare a glance in that direction.

They changed trains in Paris, which involved traveling by hansom cab to another station for the Cherbourg train. Thus it was around late afternoon and several hours before sailing time that they found themselves—weary, dirty, and hungry—standing on the dock, gazing up at the *Titanic*.

The sheer size of the ocean liner took Aria's breath away. It reminded her of the huge buildings in New York City that filled a city block and soared stories into the air. Light shone from hundreds of windows, beckoning cheerfully.

"This way, this way," their porter barked, shoving a path through the crowd toward the tender—a small boat that would ferry them to the *Titanic*, which was too big for Cherbourg's docks—for them and their luggage. There was a chill breeze, and

Aria drew the fur collar of her overcoat closer around her throat.

Daisy grabbed her arm. "Don't look now, but that's John Jacob Astor and his new bride over there." She nodded to their right, at the people waiting to board.

Aria remembered the papers and society gossips had all been abuzz the year before when the middle-aged millionaire got a divorce and married a girl of eighteen. Keeping her face forward, she discreetly slid her gaze over to the couple. Astor wasn't terribly tall, but he was handsome and well groomed. His wife was devastatingly pretty, with high-piled dark hair and a trim figure. With them were a man and woman whom Aria guessed were servants, judging by their black clothing and the way they walked behind the Astors. The man glanced her way, and when his intense dark eyes met hers, Aria was stunned by his chiseled good looks. He gave her a brisk nod and quickly turned away.

"Oh look." Daisy was craning her neck toward another passenger. "Lady Duff-Gordon, our dress designer! I didn't know she was sailing with us." She clapped her gloved hands, pleased as any child with a new toy. "I guess the papers were right when they said many prominent people were on the passenger list for *Titanic*'s maiden voyage. I'm thrilled to be here among them."

As first-class passengers, they were ushered through a set of double doors and into a reception room. When Aria gave their names to the steward, another man stepped forward with a bow. "Good evening, Miss Griffin, Miss Greco. I am Mr. Pierce, the assistant purser for First Class. I will show you to your suite." Tall, with blond hair and a mustache, he had dark-blue eyes and an English accent.

This was special treatment indeed. The assistant purser was quite high in the ship's service hierarchy.

"Thank you, Mr. Pierce." Daisy gave him one of her brilliant smiles. "Please do show us the way. I am absolutely knackered, as you Brits say."

"How about you, Miss Greco? Are you knackered as well?"

To Aria's surprise, the purser gave her a warm smile and a nod as he stood back to let them pass into the corridor. She was used to being invisible when escorting Daisy. "I am fine. It was a long journey, however. All the way from Monte Carlo."

"Ah. Lovely place." He strode ahead of them. "You are on B deck, with the rest of the staterooms. Right this way."

He led them through a maze of hallways to the graceful grand staircase, embellished with carved wood, a huge glass dome to let in light, and bronze cherubs holding lamps. Even Daisy couldn't repress a gasp at its beauty.

"It's something, isn't it?" Mr. Pierce said. "Lovely as any top-class hotel."

Aria gazed around, drinking in every detail. The setting would be perfect for a movie scene. *Perhaps a shipboard romance.* She could imagine her male lead waiting at the bottom for his ladylove to descend the staircase . . .

At the bottom of one flight, the purser led them down a corridor almost to the end. "You are fortunate to get this suite," Mr. Pierce said as he unlocked the door and opened it wide, standing aside to let them enter. "This is where the White Star Line really outdid itself, I feel."

Aria had to agree. With carved woodwork, flocked wallpaper, and period furnishings, the two bedrooms, parlor, wardrobe room, and bath were nicer than any shipboard accommodations she had seen. Daisy's room had a curtained bed, like that in an English manor house, and Aria's had twin beds. Heaters, fans, and seaworthy lamps completed the outfit.

"Here's the call button," Mr. Pierce said. "Press this anytime, day or night, and someone will come to serve you."

"Will they bring food?" Daisy asked. "I'm too tired to dine out tonight."

The purser bowed. "Of course. Anything you wish."

"Hot soup and bread and a bottle of wine would be fine. What do you think, Aria?"

"That's fine with me, thanks." The trunks had arrived, and Aria was directing their placement in the wardrobe room. Considering the size of Daisy's wardrobe, the oversize closet was a very useful feature.

Aria heard the door close behind the purser and the porters. Daisy appeared in the doorway of the wardrobe room. "Will you be a love and pull out my negligee? I want to bathe before we eat."

"I'd like to do that too." Aria couldn't wait to change out of her creased and limp garments and wash the train's grime from her face and hands.

"I'll save you some hot water, although I'll bet this ship has plenty." Daisy disappeared into the other room.

Aria knelt on the carpet and opened the lid of the trunk holding Daisy's undergarments and nightgowns. The pink negligee was on the bottom, of course, so Aria had to rummage around.

Her hand banged against something hard. *Ouch.* What was that? Groping around, she managed to grab the object, which was smooth and cold. It felt like—but how could it be? She pulled the item out and stared at it in horrified disbelief. What on earth was Daisy doing with a revolver?

5

Corinna, Vermont
Present Day

At Julie's words, panic jolted Sofia. Had Ian drowned in the lake? Squinting her eyes, she frantically searched the bright water, lapping so innocently against the dock. She couldn't see anything floating nearby, and she was thankful that there was no sign of a body.

Marla appeared on the lawn, barefoot, still wearing her T-shirt and boxers. "What's going on?" she called.

"Check to see if Ian's car is still here," Sofia called back. "We don't know where he is."

Marla darted across the grass to the rear of the cottage, where they had parked. Within seconds she was back, nodding her head. The car was still there, so he hadn't left that way. Sofia gestured for Marla to come down to the dock, where Julie was slumped, hands over her face.

Sofia quickly filled Marla in and asked her to stay with Julie. "Maybe he took a walk down the shoreline path. I'll go look." She would also check the bank to see if he had washed up somewhere else, but there was no need to share that theory with his sister.

Marla sat on the dock beside Julie and put her arm around her friend. Gazing up at Sofia, she nodded. "I'll wait here."

Sofia wished she had stopped to put on shoes as she trotted down the dirt path, which was scattered with some pine needles and grass. She stepped on rocks and roots a few times, but she ignored the pain and kept going. Action was better than allowing the idea that Ian was dead to settle in. It was just too horrible to contemplate. He *had* to be here somewhere.

She passed her cottage and several others. No sign of life anywhere. All turned blank windows to the shore. Covered boats rocked gently at their berths, and boathouse doors were padlocked shut. Far out on the water, a fishing boat trolled along, its motor barely discernible despite the early morning hush.

At the end of the point, the path petered out into woods, with no sign of anyone pushing through the thicket that faced her. She turned back, walking more slowly. There was no evidence of him anywhere along the path and only a swampy inlet lay in the other direction from Julie's camp. Had he left the cottage some other way? Maybe a friend picked him up. But then why leave clothing and shoes on the dock? She recognized them as the ones he had been wearing the night before.

"Any sign of him?" Marla called as Sofia approached Julie's cottage.

Sofia ran to join her friends. "No. I went all the way to the end of the point." She and Marla exchanged significant glances, certainty growing. "I think we'd better call the police."

At her words, Julie gave a wail. "No, oh no! What could have happened?"

"We don't know yet," Marla said gently. "Let's go up to the house."

Getting to her feet, Julie reached to gather up Ian's belongings, but Sofia said, "Leave them. The police need to see them exactly the way they were."

Julie's eyes widened, and she clapped a hand over her mouth. With a muffled groan, she ran for the house. Sofia and Marla followed on her heels.

"I don't blame her," Marla said. "I could throw up myself."

"This is horrible," Sofia said. "I hope it's all a misunderstanding."

Inside, Sofia placed the call while Marla got Julie settled on the living room sofa. The dispatcher was skeptical until Sofia repeated the information about Ian's clothes on the dock.

While she waited for an officer to arrive, Sofia put coffee on and made toast. She heard a low murmur as Julie spoke to Mark on the phone in the living room.

Marla entered the room, wearing jeans and a T-shirt. "I'll take over if you want to get dressed."

Sofia glanced down at her sleep shirt and boxers. "Yeah, I suppose I should before the police show up." She headed for the stairs.

Tires crunched on gravel just as Sofia came back downstairs. Marla was still with Julie, so Sofia answered the back door.

A Caucasian female displayed her badge and said, "Officer Quimby, Corinna police." She jerked a thumb at her partner, an African-American male standing next to her. "That's Officer Jackson. Someone here called about a missing person?"

Officer Quimby . . . Could it be? Sofia studied the woman's broad, freckled face and sturdy build. "Are you related to Ryan Quimby of the Cabot Falls Police Department, by any chance?"

Surprise flitted across Officer Quimby's impassive face. "That's right. I'm his cousin, Roxanne. And you are?"

"Sofia Parker. I live in Cabot Falls. Ryan's a good friend. And a good cop." For Sofia, the connection to a policeman they knew and trusted helped her feel more confident.

"Yeah, Ryan's a great guy," Office Quimby said. "And yes, I'd say that even if I wasn't related to him." She grinned. "I don't see him very often since we're both so busy, but tell him I said hey."

"I'll do that. Please, come in." Sofia stood back to let the officers enter.

"Is the missing person related to you?" Officer Jackson asked.

Sofia shook her head. "No. Julie Butler's family owns this cottage. The missing man, Ian Marshall, is her brother."

Sofia led the officers into the living room and introduced Julie and Marla to the officers. Even the distraught Julie was obviously surprised at the name Quimby.

Hands on hips, Officer Jackson gazed around the room. "Take me through it, step by step, Mrs. Butler." His voice was a warm grumble.

Julie explained how, after she had gotten up, she had looked for Ian in the bunk room, where he said he was going to stay. After not finding him there, or any of the four bunks disturbed, she went out to see if he was on the front porch daybed, where people sometimes slept, when she spotted something on the dock: his clothing and shoes.

"His car is still here," she finished tearfully. "So he must have gone swimming and drowned."

"We don't know that, ma'am," Officer Quimby said. The officers exchanged looks. "Which car is his?"

"The sedan," Marla said.

"I'll run plates." Officer Jackson made a note on his cell phone. "Let's go take a look at the dock."

Julie led the way to the dock, seemingly energized by the arrival of someone to listen and help. She pointed to the clothes. "As I got closer, I could see those were Ian's. I recognized that red polo shirt."

Sofia and Marla hung back while Officers Quimby and Jackson examined the clothing without touching it. They conferred in low tones, then Officer Quimby set off toward the cruiser.

"We'll have to take these clothes into evidence," Officer Jackson said. "And we'll get the Marine Patrol out here to look for him."

Sofia was startled. "You're treating this like a crime?"

"That's right. Until we . . . uh, gather more information, we can't rule out foul play."

Sofia guessed he had been going to say "recover the body" and appreciated his discretion.

Poised to continue taking notes, Officer Jackson turned to Julie. "About what time did you come down here? And what time was it when you last saw him?"

Julie gave the answers, barely able to hold back tears. After Officer Jackson finished, Marla asked, "Do you mind if we go inside?"

"That's fine," the officer said. "Just don't go anywhere, okay?"

Marla and Julie went back up to the cottage, accompanied by Officer Quimby, but Sofia stayed outside, moving where she could watch but not interfere. She perched on an Adirondack chair and called Jim.

Vanessa answered. "Hi, Mom. It's me. You know how Dad is about talking on the cell phone in the car."

Sofia forced a laugh. "And you should follow his example. I take it you're on your way up here?"

"Yes. We left about an hour ago. Do you need me to give Dad a message?"

Sofia thought quickly. She certainly didn't want to pass along the bad news via her daughter. Besides, maybe Ian would turn up and this emergency would become a Butler family fable often retold.

"Mom? Are you still there?" Vanessa's voice was anxious. "I sure hope I can get reception up there. I'm expecting some important calls."

Sofia heard Jim laugh in the background. *Oh, for the troubles of a teenager.* "I'm here, honey. Just tell him to give me a call when you stop for a break. Nothing urgent."

"I will. Love you."

Officer Quimby came back down to the shore, and shortly thereafter, a crime scene tech joined the officers and took photographs before searching through the jeans pockets, which appeared to be empty. She made a confused face and conferred with the others, who also looked concerned, before putting the clothing and shoes into evidence bags.

Officer Quimby came across the grass to Sofia. “Ms. Parker, I have a question for you. Have you seen Ian Marshall’s cell phone or wallet?”

Hope made Sofia’s pulse leap. If Ian was like most young people, he was never more than a few feet away from his phone. “They weren’t in his pants?”

“Apparently not. Unless you or one of the other ladies removed them.”

“I didn’t. And I don’t think Julie or Marla did.” Then her bubble of hope deflated. “Maybe he left them in the house or in his car.”

“Maybe. Let’s hope not.” The officer’s eyes met Sofia’s, a look of understanding passing between them. Officer Quimby was also keeping her fingers crossed that Ian Marshall was alive and well somewhere.

While the adults sat on the porch, attempting to eat a late lunch, the Parker boys, Tim Dixon, and the Butler twins were playing in the water with shouts and screams of pleasure and enjoyment, accompanied by a jubilant Fergus. Vanessa and Wynter were sunning on the floating dock a short distance from shore.

“He must be alive,” Julie said for about the tenth time. “So why isn’t he answering his phone?” She slammed her cell phone down on the table.

Mark Butler put his arm around his wife's shoulders and squeezed. "I don't know, but if he's not dead, I'll kill him when he does show up." His rather lame joke elicited wan smiles from the other adults. "I hope the police will be able to triangulate his cell signal and find him."

Jim set down a pair of binoculars he was using to study boats on the lake. "Looks like the Marine Patrol is still out searching," he whispered to Sofia.

Sofia bit her lip, thinking about what Officer Quimby had said. Although the police had failed to find Ian's cell phone or wallet, they weren't ready to call off the search just yet.

Marla got up from the table. "I'm going to make another pitcher of iced tea."

Sofia also stood. "How about some iced gingerbread cookies to go with it? I brought some."

As if lured by the very mention of cookies, Matthew appeared at the screen door, soaking wet, wrapped in a towel, his teeth chattering. "Can I have a snack, Mom?"

"Of course," Sofia said. "Ask the others if they want one."

He ran off, shouting, and Sofia slipped into the cool, dimly lit house to get the cookies. In the kitchen, she found Marla adding ice cubes to the large, clear pitcher.

"The tension is killing me," Marla said. "I can't imagine how Julie feels."

"Me neither. Where can Ian be? What is he doing? It just doesn't make sense." Sofia located the plastic tub holding the gingerbread cookies and pulled off the lid.

"No it doesn't." Marla pulled a jug of tea out of the refrigerator and began pouring it into the pitcher. "I find it hard to believe that he would worry his sister like this intentionally."

"Me too. He must know that she's worried sick." Sofia placed some cookies on a platter, arranging them in a neat formation despite knowing it would be demolished in seconds once the ravenous horde descended. She picked up the plate. "Ready?"

They were halfway back to the porch when they heard shouting. In one accord, they sped up, almost losing the tea and cookies in the process.

Sofia burst through the porch door. "What is it?"

Julie was both laughing and crying. She jabbed a forefinger at the table but was unable to talk. Sofia saw nothing new, just the remnants of lunch and several cell phones lined up where the kids had left them before going swimming.

Mark spoke for his wife. "Ian texted Ellie. He's alive."

Titanic
April 10, 1912

Aria tucked the gun away with shaking fingers, discovering a small sack of bullets in the process. She could scarcely believe the lighthearted and gentle Daisy had kept such a secret from her or even that she possessed a firearm. Inseparable since childhood, Aria thought they told each other everything. Well, almost everything. She herself had a few secrets, mainly her conversation with Pierre Lafitte.

Finding the gun rocked Aria, making her question everything she had taken for granted. Then fear stabbed. *Is Daisy in danger?* Perhaps she didn't want to involve Aria. That would be like Daisy, trying to shield her friend.

She dug the gun out from among the froth of undergarments again. The only way forward was to ask for the truth. Their friendship required no less.

Daisy was in her cabin, stripped down to chemise and drawers. "Did you find my nightgown?" Her gaze fell on the object Aria held cradled in both hands. "Oh."

Aria gently set it on the dresser and clasped her hands tightly at her waist. "Daisy, why do you have a gun?"

Daisy slumped onto the bed. "I thought I needed it." She glanced up at Aria, her blue eyes wide and pleading. "I didn't want to trouble you."

"Trouble me? You know everything that concerns you concerns me! How could you keep such a secret? And why?"

Daisy's eyes went to the flowered carpet, and she traced the pattern with her toe. "It is a matter I wish to forget."

Illumination dawned. "Is it something to do with Pierre Lafitte?"

A couple of months ago, just before they were going to start another film with the director, something had happened between Daisy and Pierre that resulted in Daisy refusing to work with him again. But Daisy steadfastly refused to give Aria the details.

Daisy bit her lip, a sign she was thinking furiously. Emotions washed over her face: fear, doubt, a flash of anger, then firm resolution. "It might have something to do with him." She held up a hand. "No, I'm not going to say more about . . . that night. So please don't ask." She swallowed hard. "You know that note I got at the hotel? It wasn't the only one."

Aria pulled the bench from the dressing table and sat. "You've had other threatening notes?"

Daisy shrugged. "Two. The first was in Paris right after the Pierre incident. The second was at the hotel, right after we got there."

Aria was outraged that she hadn't found the messages or been told about them. "Where was I? I usually handle the mail."

"They came when you were out." Correctly guessing Aria's next question, she added, "I ripped them up and threw them away." To demonstrate, she tore invisible paper into tiny shreds.

"Oh, Daisy. We should have taken them to the *gendarme*."

Daisy's gaze was evasive. "But why? They were only words on paper."

Aria gestured at the gun. "You purchased *that*, so obviously they bothered you."

Daisy bit her lip again. "True," she finally admitted. She pushed down on the bed to stand. "But let's forget about it, all right? I overreacted to someone's cowardly nonsense and bought the gun.

I'll sell it in New York. Right now, I want a bath, dinner, and bed."

Aria reluctantly got to her feet. "I'll go look for your negligee."

Daisy could tell her to forget about the gun, but she wasn't going to. Somehow she would figure out who sent the notes and why. And what terrible thing had taken place between Daisy and that scoundrel, Pierre Lafitte.

Loud blasts sounded. The *Titanic* was leaving port.

The enormous ship glided smoothly through quiet waters, engines thrumming, and consequently, Aria enjoyed a good night's sleep in her plush stateroom. The next morning, after putting on a robe and slippers, she entered Daisy's room to find the actress already awake.

"I've ordered breakfast," Daisy said. She was sitting up in bed, glancing through a booklet. "It should be here any moment."

Aria stretched with a yawn. "What do you want to do today?"

"I've heard we're stopping briefly in Ireland to take on more passengers later this morning. Supposedly there will be Irish merchants on board."

"That might be worth a look. I need to get some air and stretch my legs." After traveling for two days, Aria felt stiff and restless.

Daisy waved a page at her. "According to this, there's a gymnasium on a lower deck."

"That sounds like too much exercise, although I wouldn't mind a swim. There's a pool, isn't there?"

"Yes. And Turkish baths. I want to indulge in one of those." Daisy shivered with pleasure. "This voyage is going to be like an extension of our vacation."

Perhaps, as long as they could avoid Pierre and there were no more threatening notes.

Someone knocked on the parlor door, and Aria hurried to answer. She was eager for a cup of coffee, a habit she had gotten used to in France. The United States imported coffee too, but no one made it like the Europeans.

To her surprise, Mr. Pierce, the assistant purser, stood there, holding a tray. "Good morning, Miss Greco."

"Served by the assistant purser. I'm impressed."

Had the purser assigned Mr. Pierce to take care of them? She wouldn't mind that at all. Standing aside, she watched as he entered the room and set a tray on the table, which held two covered plates that he set in place. He poured coffee from a tall silver pot into two cups. Glasses of juice and a rack of toast completed the meal. Copies of the ship newspaper, the *Atlantic Daily Bulletin*, sat next to each plate.

"When you're finished, you can put the tray and dishes outside the room, and someone will collect it." He stood at attention, giving his heels a slight click together. "Is there anything else, Miss Greco?"

"That's it, I think. Thank you."

He lingered a moment. "Miss Greco, I was wondering . . ."

Her heart began to thud. "Yes, Mr. Pierce?"

"I'd be happy to give you a tour of the ship. The full tour, if you're interested."

"I'd like that, Mr. Pierce."

He smiled, his blue eyes crinkling. "Lovely. Are you free this afternoon, say around two?"

Aria pretended to think about it. "I believe so."

"Meet me at the Grand Staircase clock." He gave her a quick salute. "See you then, Miss Greco."

Daisy emerged as soon as the door closed behind Mr. Pierce.

"What was all that about?" She sat at the table and took the lid off her plate. "Ooh. These scrambled eggs look perfect."

Aria joined her at the table. "Mr. Pierce is going to give me a tour of the ship, a real tour. I hope that includes the bridge, if the captain doesn't mind."

Daisy wrinkled her nose. "Why would you want to see all that?" She poured cream into her coffee and stirred, then took a sip.

Why indeed? Yes, she was fascinated by everything about the ocean liner, but secretly, her excitement had more to do with Mr. Pierce. She wasn't going to admit that to Daisy. A White Star Line employee was too lowly to contemplate in her eyes—unless he was the captain, maybe.

"I'm gathering material for a scenario," she said, taking a nibble of toast. That excuse served to cover a multitude of situations, she had learned.

Daisy pursed her lips. "A likely story. Mr. Pierce is a very handsome young man, even if he is merely a purser."

"We can't all be courted by millionaires or lords," Aria said.

"Don't sell yourself short, Aria. You are beautiful, even if you persist in doubting it." She tapped her head. "Think less and *feel* more. You'll have men falling at your feet."

Aria giggled at the image Daisy's words created. "As long as they don't get in my way, I don't mind." She took a deep breath. Maybe she should stop working so hard and try to enjoy herself. She was in a first-class cabin on the most acclaimed ship in the world, in company with captains of industry, English nobility, and a famous dress designer. How marvelous was that?

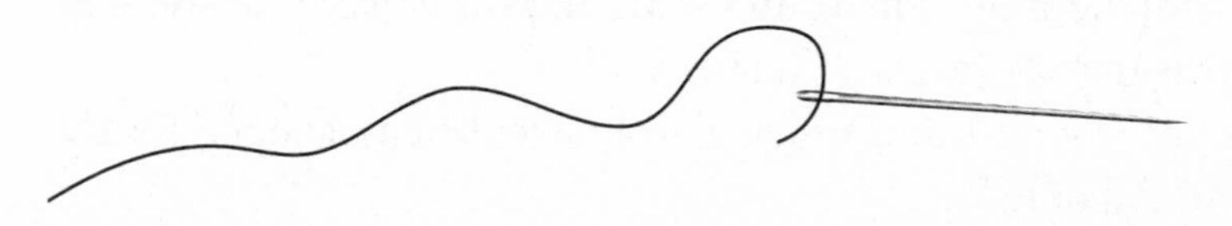

"I'm glad I wore my overcoat," Aria said as she and Daisy emerged on deck a couple of hours later. She shivered, grateful for the black wool coat she wore over her lavender day dress.

"Yes, it's sunny, but that breeze is freezing. It must be coming straight down from the Arctic." Daisy also wore a coat; hers was navy blue, a color that looked nice with her white dress.

"Our route almost takes us there, I heard." Aria paused to look around the vast deck. Passengers were strolling, lounging in deck chairs, or thronged around the tables holding Irish wares. Overhead, the huge smokestacks loomed, emitting streams of black smoke. A short distance across the water, Aria could see the buildings of Queenstown, Ireland, dogged tenders plowing through the waves as they ferried passengers and their luggage to the ship. Their last sight of land until North America.

"I want to look at the lace," Aria said. "My mother loves using it in her shop. Maybe I'll buy some for her."

"You are such a thoughtful daughter," Daisy said. "I should send my mother a new tablecloth. Irish linen is some of the best in the world."

They pushed through the crowd to the tables. "We have the finest lace made on the Emerald Isle," one woman called out to them. She held up a lace collar. "Handmade, every stitch."

Aria recognized the work as Youghal lace, made with a needle and thread finer than a human hair, rather than with a bobbin like many lovely laces. Inspired by Italian designs, lace from this region was worn by royalty, including Queen Mary. Aria's mother would love it.

"What else do you have?" Aria asked. The woman obligingly brought out more collars and some lengths of lace that could be used as trim or insets. "I'll take it all."

The woman's eyes widened in amazement and hope. "Really, mum? All of it?"

"Yes. What's your price?" Aria reached for the little purse she kept tucked in a pocket.

A sum was named, absurdly low. "I'll give you this much." Aria placed a pile of pound notes in the woman's outstretched hand. Due to their travels, she ended up carrying British, French, and American money.

Daisy threw Aria an amused glance. "That's double what she asked," she whispered. "You're not much of a bargainer, are you?"

"No, I'm not. Besides, it's well worth it." Aria knew that the lace makers were mostly poor rural women trying to support their families. Babbling gratitude and blessings, the woman packed the lace gently in a linen pillowcase and handed it to Aria.

"On to the linen," Daisy said, "now that you've cleaned out the lace." As Daisy turned and began to work through the crowd, she gasped, putting one gloved hand to her lips.

Aria followed her gaze. Pierre Lafitte was heading their way, dapper in a derby hat and wool overcoat, jauntily swinging a cane. He gave each woman he passed a smile of appreciation and a tip of his hat.

Daisy turned, bumping into Aria. "Let's go this way. I suddenly don't feel well." Her face was dead white under her rouge, which stood out like bright circles.

"What is it, dearie?" a woman in the crowd asked. "A touch of seasickness?"

"That's right," Daisy said. "I'm seasick." Bending over slightly, she clutched her belly, allowing Aria to guide her off the deck. Once they were safely inside a reception area empty except for potted palms and seating groups, she took Aria's arm, eyes wide with fear. "I can't believe that man is on this boat. I'm trapped with him until we get to New York."

Aria's mouth went dry. She hadn't told Daisy about her encounter with Pierre on the train, hoping that through some miracle, they wouldn't see him during the voyage. How foolish of her. Staring out the window to the deck, she mumbled, "I should have told you."

"Speak up. You should have told me what?"

"I saw Pierre on the Paris train." Aria gave a brief description of her encounter with Pierre in the dining car, omitting his offer to hire her if she coerced Daisy back into the Pan-Francais contract.

Daisy's fists clenched, and she stamped one foot. "You saw him on the train, and you didn't think to mention it to me?"

"I'm sorry, Daisy. I didn't want to upset you. I was hoping we wouldn't run into him." She shrugged, throwing up both hands. "Stupid of me, I know."

Daisy was silent as she stared out the window at the passersby on deck.

"Should we get off the boat?" Aria suggested. They could always sail on the next ship. Then the ship's horns blasted, warning the world that the anchor was being raised and they would be on their way. "I guess it's too late."

In a sudden change of mood, Daisy whirled around, laughing. "Don't worry about it, silly. It's not your fault." Daisy took Aria's arm and leaned close. "No more secrets, all right?"

Aria swallowed. "No more secrets."

Daisy gave her arm a tug. "Come on, let's take the lace to the stateroom and then change for lunch. Perhaps we can track Edward down. He'll keep Pierre at bay for me." She brightened. "Maybe I can have him send Pierre nasty legal letters. That would be entertaining."

Aria closed her eyes briefly, releasing a sigh of relief. Maybe everything really would be all right. She just had to avoid Pierre until they got to New York.

Daisy insisted they change for lunch, and when they arrived at the intimate à la carte restaurant on B deck, she was glad they had. The women dining at the linen-covered tables were dressed befitting a tea dance rather than a luncheon.

At the doorway, Aria paused to twitch the skirt of her pale-peach gown into place and touch her hat, making sure it was firmly pinned. With amusement, she noticed Daisy doing the same to her striking outfit of blue-and-white print with a knee-length white overskirt and matching hat. Preparations of women going into battle.

"Table for two?" the formally dressed maître d' asked.

Daisy scanned the room. "We'll be joining Mr. Thurston's party." Edward and his mother were seated in an alcove on the far side of the room.

He bowed. "Very good, madam. Follow me."

Edward jumped up as they approached. "Daisy, Aria. I'm so glad you could join us. Mother, isn't it grand?" Edward helped Daisy sit down while the maître d' assisted Aria.

"Grand indeed," Edith said drily as the maître d' handed Aria and Daisy the daily menu. "Try the turtle soup," she said to Aria behind one hand. "I've heard that's grand too."

Aria repressed a smile and studied the menu. Lobster, duckling, and lamb were some of the choices, fine fare indeed. If she wasn't careful, she would need to let out her corset—again. An elegant waiter with a refined British accent came to take their orders and pour them each a glass of white wine.

Aria drank sparingly, remembering her rendezvous with Mr. Pierce that afternoon. The last thing she wanted was to become sleepy and lethargic. How did the upper classes manage to put away so much during meals? It wasn't uncommon for them to serve several different wines at dinner.

Edith's strident tones broke into her thoughts. "Tell me, Miss Greco, what do you think of the ship?"

Aria glanced across the table, noticing that Edward and Daisy were engrossed in conversation. Although they remained sitting well apart in the interests of propriety, anyone observing could practically feel Edward's intensity as he stared at Daisy. *Rather like a hawk eyeing a delectable rabbit*, Aria thought. She pushed down her discomfort and turned back to Edith.

"I think the *Titanic* is absolutely spectacular," she said. "I am enjoying the voyage very much." *With the exception of fending off Pierre Lafitte and watching Edward swoop in for the kill.*

Edith preened, as though she were responsible for the ship's success herself. "I agree with you, my dear. So much so, I think I will make it my ship for our annual European trips." She glanced around the room. "All the best people are here, I see. We have the same good taste."

Edward raised Daisy's hands to his lips. Daisy was beaming. Had they missed something vital?

"How are you two doing over there?" Aria called.

The millionaire hastily released Daisy's hand. "I'm sorry, we're being rude. We were just discussing meeting for dinner and dancing this evening."

No proposal then. Aria hid her relief by taking a sip of wine.

Beside her, Edith sighed. "No dancing for me." She sat back to let the waiter set a bowl of steaming soup in front of her. The turtle, Aria noticed. "After dinner, I'll retire early with a book."

Feeling a sudden kinship with the woman, Aria leaned close. "So will I." She didn't have the energy to go out almost every night like Daisy. With a sudden stab of hunger, Aria picked up her spoon. The Crème du Barry cauliflower soup smelled wonderful.

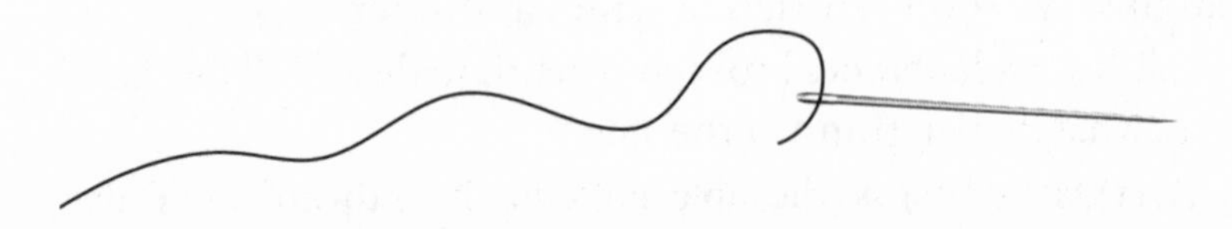

At two o'clock precisely, Aria climbed the Grand Staircase to the top landing, where she found Mr. Pierce, who beamed down at her as she ascended the final steps.

"Good afternoon, Miss Greco." They shook hands. "I'm so pleased you could join me."

"I'm pleased that you're giving me a tour. I must admit I'm curious about the rest of the ship. I haven't seen anything but first class and the deck, lovely as they are."

He gestured for Aria to proceed first. "Let's start at the top, then. The bridge."

Excitement hummed in Aria's veins as they stepped into what she knew was the brain of the ship. The room was quite large and lined with windows, composed of two wings to the side and a large wheel and compass, called a binnacle, in the center. As they strolled across the polished floor, an older man with a beard and dressed in uniform turned.

Captain Edward John Smith.

Mr. Pierce made the introductions, and Captain Smith kindly gave Aria a tour of the bridge; the wheel room, where the ship was actually controlled; and the navigation center. The wheel on the bridge was for quick maneuvers, she learned. Ahead of the boat was endless sea, marked by rippling waves. Aria felt like a bird flying over the ocean.

"How fast are we moving?" she asked.

The captain flashed a proud smile. "We're holding about twenty knots. We might even get you to New York early, young lady."

"I'm in no hurry," Aria said. "I'm finding the ship and its amenities delightful."

"The White Star Line's managing director would be happy to hear you say that. Mr. Ismay is also sailing with us." The captain paused. "Will you do me the honor of joining me at my table tomorrow night?"

Aria felt a rush of pleasure. Dining with the captain was the highest mark of favor. "I'd love to, Captain."

She and Mr. Pierce took their leave, and as they left the bridge, Aria whispered, "Thank you for that. I loved the tour, and I am thrilled to dine with the captain."

Smiling, Mr. Pierce cocked an eyebrow. "Glad I could be of assistance."

"Where are we going next?" Aria didn't think anything could top the bridge.

"To see everything this fine ship has to offer." His blue eyes regarded her anxiously. "If you're interested."

"Yes, I am. Lead on!" Frankly, Aria would have toured anything in company with the dashing Mr. Pierce.

"We'll start at the bottom and work our way up."

Mr. Pierce was true to his word. Their first stop, deep in the bowels of the ship, was the hold. It held a fascinating array of cargo, including a Renault automobile. Then they toured third class, filled with families enjoying their voyage. Second class was also quite nice, with accommodations that would be considered first class on any other ship.

"Mr. Ismay prides himself on comfortable travel for all, no matter their pocketbook," Mr. Pierce said as they climbed up to the next deck. "That's one reason I'm proud to work for White Star Line."

"Has the White Star Line been your entire career?"

"Yes, it has, so far. A nice opportunity for a young man from King's Lynn."

"Where's that?" Aria paused for breath on the landing.

"Norfolk. My dad was a farmer, and my mother took in stitching. I used to look out at the North Sea and tell myself I would sail the oceans someday."

"And here you are." She remembered something he'd said.

"My mother is also a seamstress. She lives in Boston, in an area called Little Italy. It reminds her of home. She and my father grew up in Italy." Aria began climbing again.

They chatted about their childhoods as they toured the hospital, post office, swimming pool, wireless office, and gymnasium. He took her into the kitchens, where she glimpsed vast numbers of staff running around chopping food, cooking at huge ranges, and washing dishes.

"Our stock includes forty tons of potatoes and forty thousand eggs," Mr. Pierce said. "In addition to more than thirteen hundred passengers, there are almost nine hundred crew members."

"It's like feeding an army," Aria said. "Or a small town."

"That's right." Mr. Pierce held the swinging door open for her. "Only we can't exactly order more provisions, so we have to make do with what we have and pray we don't run out."

They had entered the first-class area of the ship near the dining saloon, deserted at this hour, when they heard raised voices around a corner.

Mr. Pierce frowned. "Wait here, Miss Greco." He strode ahead, apparently planning to intervene.

She edged closer, curious. A familiar voice said quite plainly, "If dueling weren't illegal, I would call you out, sir."

It was Lord Henry.

7

Corinna, Vermont
Present Day

Sofia hastily set the cookies on the table before they spilled. "Ian texted Ellie?"

Julie held up Ellie's pink cell phone. "Yes, thank God." She glanced at the screen. "He said, 'Tell your mom I'm all right. Out of town for a few days. Don't worry.'"

"I wonder why he texted her and not you," Marla said. Ice cubes rattling, she poured iced tea into the glasses on the table.

Julie touched the screen. "I don't think he has my new number. Maybe that's why he hasn't been answering." She put Ellie's phone to her ear. "Come on, Ian, answer." After a moment, she made a face. "Straight to voice mail."

The children, led by Matthew, charged onto the porch, so the adults changed the subject. Once they ran back outside, Jim said, "We need to call the police and tell them he's alive." He gestured toward the water, where the Marine Patrol was slowly trolling by. "They're still out there searching."

"That's assuming that it was Ian who did the texting," Sofia pointed out.

"That's true," Jim said, "but I still think we need to let the authorities know."

Julie made a face. "They won't be happy, but you're absolutely right." She picked up her phone and stepped into the house, muttering, "If he only knew what havoc he was causing . . ."

Mark shook his head. "I love Ian, but he always seems to be in trouble. The proverbial bad penny, I'm sorry to say." He took a sip of his tea and stared into space, a glum look on his face.

"Look at it this way," Marla said. "Now we can start enjoying our vacation." She set the pitcher down on the table. "I think I'm going to put on my suit and take a dip." Humming, she went into the house.

Sofia slumped into her wicker chair, frosty glass in hand. The relief that Ian was alive and seemingly all right was so strong, she almost felt dizzy. But something niggled. Why hadn't he told his sister he was leaving? And how did he leave?

Jim sat beside her. "I still think there's something off about the whole situation. It doesn't add up."

"I agree."

"How did it go?" Mark asked as Julie stepped back out onto the porch and sat beside her husband.

Julie set her phone on the table. "Not too bad, considering. They were glad to hear he's all right. But I could tell by Officer Quimby's tone that she was a little ticked that the department put so many resources into searching for someone who isn't actually missing." She shook her head with a frown. "I think Ian better stay out of her way for a while."

"He better stay out of mine too," Mark said. "I can't believe he put you through that." He slung an arm around Julie's shoulders and pulled her close. "But let's forget about that. We have better things to do, like enjoy the lake and being here with our friends." He whispered something in Julie's ear, and she laughed.

Sofia leaned closer to her husband. "Why don't we go over to the cottage and put on our bathing suits? I'm ready for a swim too." She'd moved her bags over to Windward when Jim and the kids had arrived.

Jim jumped up with a grin. "Last one in is a rotten egg."

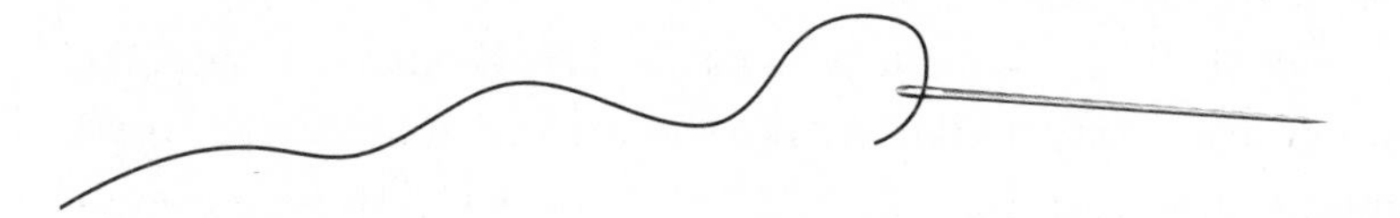

Sofia had a blast playing Marco Polo with Jim and the kids. After that, she climbed up on the floating dock and lay beside her sunbathing daughters. They chatted lightly about dates and boys and new clothes, reminding Sofia of similar long summer days with her sisters, Gina and Rosa.

As the sun lowered, making long, dark shadows in the woods, Mark and Jim fired up the barbecues. Tonight's feast was hamburgers and hot dogs, the children's favorites. Sofia had put together potato salad earlier, and Julie was making a tossed salad. For dessert, they were going to have a sundae bar with various toppings.

They were all sitting around the long table eating dinner, Fergus lurking underneath for dropped treats, when Sofia noticed a middle-aged man along the shoreline. "Is that someone you know?" she asked Mark.

Mark glanced up. "That's Bob Thompson. He owns the next cottage just beyond Windward."

Noticing the group on the porch, Bob changed course and came up to the house. "Howdy, folks." He gave a wave. "Good to see you."

"Same here, Bob," Mark said before making introductions.

Bob gazed at the shoreline, taking his cap off briefly to scratch his head.

"Is there something I can help you with, Bob?" Mark asked.

The man hesitated. "Actually, there is. I just got up here tonight, and when I was checking out the property, I noticed the boathouse was open."

"I heard there have been break-ins recently," Mark replied. "Anything missing?"

"I'm afraid so. My camping kayak." He shook his head. "You would have thought they'd take the fishing boat. That's worth something, at least. But a kayak? To most thieves, those represent nothing but a lot of hard work." He gestured at the water. "I was hoping someone just took it for a joyride and left it along the bank somewhere."

"We haven't seen it," Julie said. "But we'll keep an eye out for it. How did they get in? Did they break down the boathouse door?"

Bob made a sheepish grimace. "Nope. I stashed the padlock key up over the door. I guess I won't be doing that anymore."

"Everything all right in your cottage?" Mark asked.

"Far as I can tell." Bob adjusted his cap again. "Well, I'll leave you to your dinner." With another wave, he moved off. "Have a good night."

Sofia and Jim exchanged glances. She could practically see what he was thinking: Ian might have taken that boat. First, he probably knew about it, and second, that would explain how he left without taking his car. As soon as she could, she would share her theory with Julie. Maybe she would have an idea where Ian might have paddled.

"Speaking of boats," Mark said, "we do an annual camping trip to an island on the lake. What do you think, Parkers and Dixons?"

"Camping? Yahoo!" Matthew yelled.

Jim sent him a warning look.

"It's really fun," Ellie assured the others solemnly.

"I'd like to do that," Tim Dixon said. "At Scouts, I learned how to build a fire from scratch and build a lean-to from a tarp."

"No need of that," Mark said. "We have big tents and camping stoves." At the boy's crestfallen face, he added, "But you can build a lean-to anyway if you want. And fires only in the pit. State rules."

"Can we sleep in the lean-to, Dad?" Luke asked Jim.

"We'll see," Jim said.

"Do we paddle out?" Sofia asked. She liked boating, but that could be a real workout, depending on how far the island was. And what if they tipped over? She shuddered. Even with life jackets that was a scary thought.

Julie laughed. "Paddle? No way. We have a huge party boat. It goes about two miles an hour, but it can hold all our gear."

"I'm in, then," Marla said.

After dinner and dessert, the kids helped with cleanup, then piled into the living room to watch a movie. The adults sat on lawn chairs around the fire pit Mark and Jim built, the flickering light playing on their faces and deepening the shadows outside the circle.

"I love this," Marla said, tipping her head back to gaze at the sky. "The stars are so much brighter here than in town."

Sofia had to agree. The Milky Way made an ethereal white swath across the inky sky. "I'm excited to do some painting. Maybe tomorrow."

"The Pinot Painters strike again," Jim said with a grin.

"That's right, mister." Julie pointed at Jim in mock reproof. "We're armed with paintbrushes and should be considered dangerous."

Everyone laughed. Sofia was happy to see Julie relaxed now that she wasn't so worried about her brother.

"I'm planning on going fishing and then doing a whole lot of nothing," Mark said.

"Sounds good," Jim said. "I brought my new pole and some great lures. At least, the guy in the store said they were great."

"Let's go take a look," Mark said. "You mind, ladies?"

They all shook their heads, so he and Jim got up and wandered over to Windward, discussing their fishing plans.

"I meant to tell you," Sofia said. "I found out in one of the library books that a *Titanic* survivor, Etta Bannister, lived nearby. In Sandwich."

"That's interesting," Marla said. "Do you suppose there might still be relatives around?"

"Maybe. I thought it was worth checking out." Then she remembered something else. "Oh, and get this—Aria's friend, Daisy, was a film actress."

Julie picked up a long stick and poked at the fire to make the flames leap again. "There were film actresses in 1912? I didn't know that."

"Yes, there certainly were," Marla said, going into librarian mode. "The first film exhibition was in 1894, in New York. In 1912, films were still silent and only minutes long, but there were already a number of production companies in existence. Around that time, the industry was gradually moving out to Hollywood."

"That's fascinating," Sofia said. "I wonder if we can get some of Daisy's films."

"We'll have to check online," Julie said. "We can have them shipped here and have another movie night."

"Sounds like a plan," Sofia said.

The screen door on the porch opened. Matthew's small figure stood there, Fergus at his feet. "Mom, I'm hungry."

The trio looked at one another and laughed. "Is the movie over?" Sofia called. At his affirmative, she got up. "I guess I'll go get my horde settled."

Julie rose as well. "I should put the twins to bed. It's way past their bedtime. When you go over, can you tell Mark to come damp this fire down, Sofia?" She stretched. "Then let's get together for a cup of tea before bed. Maybe we can order Daisy's movies tonight."

"Yes to both," Sofia said. "But make mine herbal."

Marla concurred.

Sofia corralled her reluctant brood, and they trooped over to Windward. After giving them cookies and milk in the kitchen, she herded them up to their beds.

"We both get a top bunk," Matthew crowed in their room, which had two sets of bunk beds. Clad in his superhero pajamas, he scrambled up and flopped down. "I love it here."

"You're such a nerd," Luke said.

Sofia listened to their prayers and then tucked them in. As she kissed Matthew's cheek, an owl hooted outside the window.

Matthew stiffened. "What was that? It sounded scary."

Luke rolled his eyes. "It's only an owl."

In the near dark, Sofia could tell that Matthew's eyes were nearly brimming with tears. "Ellie and Cindy told me their uncle disappeared in the lake." His lower lip trembled.

Uh-oh. What made us think the kids wouldn't catch on to the Ian situation? Sofia cleared her throat. "That's not what happened, Matthew. We didn't know where he was this morning, and we were worried. But we've heard from him, and he's okay."

"Okay. I'll try not to think about it." Matthew sighed and turned on his side. "Night, Mom."

"Night, boys. Sleep tight." If only she could shed her concerns so easily. Her nerves were jangled from the shock of thinking Ian had drowned.

She checked on the girls, who were reading in their twin beds, then walked back over to Julie's cottage. Jim and Mark were standing by the fire, chatting as the coals died down. She was glad to see Jim having such a good time. Between teaching school and dealing with family needs, he didn't get much guy time.

Marla and Julie were already in the kitchen, sitting at the round oak table, waiting for the water in the kettle to boil. Julie had set out a tray of tea bags, as well as mugs, milk, sugar, honey, and lemon. Sofia joined them and started leafing through the packets.

"I'm having chamomile," Julie said. "I'm absolutely bushed, and I need a good night's sleep." The kettle whistled, and she jumped up to retrieve the boiling water.

Marla was scrolling through her phone. "Good news. I found a collection of Daisy Griffin films." She held her index finger poised. "Shall I order it? It's only on DVD." She turned the phone toward Sofia so she could see the item's price.

"Go ahead," Sofia said. "I'll pay for it." She selected a tea bag and removed it from its protective envelope.

Julie brought the kettle over and began to pour the hot water into the mugs. "And I'll pay for overnight shipping."

"It's a deal." Marla made a few more swipes, then set her phone down. "Online shopping is dangerous. I can be way too impulsive."

"Tell me about it," Julie said. She set the kettle back on the stove and returned to her chair, where she started dunking her tea bag up and down in the steaming water. "This is important, though, helping Sofia research her quilt. That's my story, and I'm sticking to it."

The night was quiet, and Sofia heard a car engine approaching down the dirt road. "Are you expecting someone else?"

Julie shook her head. "No. Maybe they're going to one of the other camps."

But the vehicle didn't pass. Instead, it pulled into the yard, engine rumbling.

Julie jumped up. "Maybe it's Ian." She went to the back door, and Sofia and Marla followed, as eager as Julie to find out who it was.

Outside, one lamp illuminated the parking area. A large, dark sedan sat there, idling. As they emerged from the cottage, both the driver's side and passenger doors opened, and two tall, muscular men stepped out.

8

Titanic
April 11, 1912

Aria recognized the growl of Lord Henry's voice threatening someone, so she edged closer to peer around the corner. Lord Henry and Edward Thurston stood nose-to-nose like angry dogs. They broke apart when Mr. Pierce left Aria's side to approach them.

"Gentlemen. May I be of assistance?" He gave a slight bow, hands clasped behind his back.

Edward threw him an irritated look and pushed past, heading toward Aria. The corridor was narrow, but he didn't seem to notice her. His eyes were fixed straight ahead, a scowl on his face.

Lord Henry tipped his hat to Mr. Pierce and strode in the opposite direction. Mr. Pierce returned to Aria, impeccably discreet, not even commenting on the altercation. He offered her his arm. "Will you join me in the Café Parisien for a cup of coffee?"

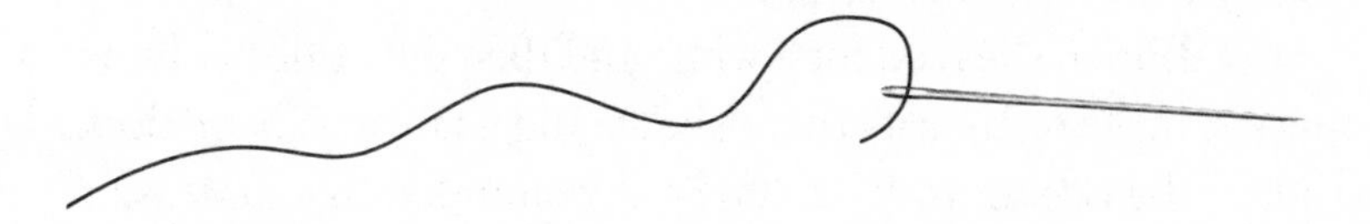

That evening, Daisy dressed in one of her best gowns and went to dinner with Edward while Aria ordered a tray brought to the stateroom. This time, a young woman with curly, pinned-up auburn hair and a fresh, rosy complexion delivered her meal, and Aria recognized her as the stewardess who had made their beds.

"Do they ever give you time off?" Aria asked as the stewardess set the tray on the table.

"Oh yes," she said, her voice lilting in an Irish brogue. Her broad smile revealed dimples in her round cheeks. "I have time off in the afternoons and then come back on in the evening."

Aria sat at the table. "What's your name?" It never felt right to her to be waited on by someone and not know a name.

"Molly at your service, miss. Is there anything else I can get you?"

Aria surveyed the bowl of soup, plate of sandwiches, and tiny pot of coffee. "No, thank you. This looks excellent." She unfolded her napkin and put it on her lap.

"I'll let myself out, then. Have a nice evening, miss."

"You too, Molly."

Aria picked up her spoon and began to eat. After the hectic events of the past few days, it felt good to be alone and relax. Her tour with Mr. Pierce had been highly enjoyable and a nice reminder that life existed outside the exalted social circles Daisy favored.

She thought again about the scene between Edward and Lord Henry. What had they been discussing so heatedly? Daisy, maybe? Perhaps a gambling debt? Either way, it just confirmed that no matter how lofty their position, people were still subject to unruly emotional displays.

After dinner, she read for a while and then put aside her book, feeling strangely restless. Perhaps she should go for a walk on deck. Gazing at the ocean under a starry sky sounded like a pleasant pursuit. In the North Atlantic there were often dense clouds, especially in April. Perhaps she would never get the opportunity for such a sight again. She put on her overcoat and added a wool scarf that could drape around her head if the wind was chilly.

They were heading into northern waters, and the air was likely becoming colder.

Making sure she had the key, she let herself out of the stateroom and headed for the stairs. The hallways were quiet, since most people were in the dining saloon or one of the other gathering places.

Out on deck, there were a few other hardy souls strolling. She made her way forward, to the very bow of the ship, and found a bench to sit on, out of the breeze. She took long breaths, drawing the sea air deeply into her lungs.

In addition to the solitude, she also cherished time spent in nature, whether woods, beaches, meadows, or the sight of silver stars twinkling in an inkblot sky a thousand miles from land. The vast ocean was equally dark, not a light to be seen anywhere. The *Titanic* was alone, forging through frigid empty waters while her people danced and dined. The contrast between the lively scene inside and the loneliness of the sea aroused a pleasurable melancholy. How could she capture that in a scenario—

"May I join you, Mademoiselle Greco?"

Icy fingers coursed down her spine. She tensed for flight. "Monsieur Lafitte."

Her cool tone didn't discourage him. He stood beside her, gazing out toward the bow. "I must apologize, mademoiselle."

Those were not words she expected to hear from his lips. "Why is that, monsieur?"

Pierre turned his head and their eyes met. "I was . . . What do the English call it? Ham-handed, that is it. I was ham-handed when I made that proposition on the train. Clumsy, an oaf, an imbecile." He knocked on his head with one fist.

Aria suppressed a giggle at his antics. Despite her reservations, she felt herself softening toward him. "I get your point, monsieur, and I accept your apology." That didn't mean, however, that she trusted him entirely. Not yet. Perhaps not ever.

He bowed, taking off his hat in a theatrical sweep. "*Merci.* Is it possible, then, for us to start again?"

Was he making another attempt at manipulating her, or rather, manipulating Daisy through her? *Only one way to find out.* "I will allow that." She moved over on the bench. "Have a seat, *s'il vous plaîs.*"

He sat with much settling of his coattails, a looming presence beside her in the near dark. He tipped his head back and regarded the sky. "Ah. You don't see stars like this in Paris."

"No, not in any city."

"You are not dancing tonight, mademoiselle? Surely a *belle femme* such as yourself would never lack for partners."

Aria shrugged. "I wanted some time alone to think. It's necessary for me to fill up the creative well that way."

"Ah, yes. The creative well. I understand." He paused a long moment. "You are a very fine writer, you know."

Pierre's words warmed her, slipping past her defenses. Self-doubt was a constant battle for writers, since it was so difficult to assess the quality of one's own writing.

"Thank you. You are kind to say so."

"Not kind. Honest. I would like you to write a scenario for me." He put up one hand. "No strings attached."

Aria's mind raced. Could she—should she trust him? Was this an elaborate ploy to lower her defenses so he could ask her again to twist Daisy's arm? She stalled by asking, "What is the topic? And what is the payment?"

Pierre chuckled. "You are forthright. I like that. I will pay you fifty dollars American."

Aria gulped. That was the top rate for scenarios. "How long?"

"Six scenes. If I like it, I may ask you to write a script. Films are getting longer, even as lengthy as an hour."

An hour! Aria could barely imagine writing something that

long. It would require an excellent plot to hold the audience's attention. Although they did sit still for plays. Films could be shot anywhere, so they weren't hampered by the limitations of a stage production.

Her heart pounding, she asked, "What is the topic?" She hoped her skills could rise to the occasion.

"Anything you wish. We can discuss it before you start writing, if you wish." He rose to his feet and tipped his hat. "I bid you good night, mademoiselle, and look forward to hearing your ideas."

"Good night, monsieur." Aria sat on the bench for a while after he left, her mind whirring with ideas. Then doubt trickled into her mind. Was this generous offer merely a trap? What payment would he exact in return? And she really shouldn't take the assignment without telling Daisy.

No more secrets—right?

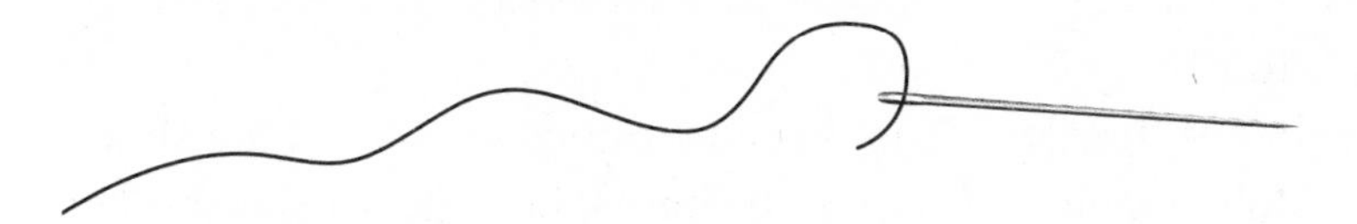

"Maybe he'll propose tonight." Daisy set aside the issue of *Harper's Bazaar* she had been perusing in the stateroom parlor.

"Edward?" Aria stopped writing, pen poised over the letter she was composing to her mother. She still hadn't decided whether to mention the lace. Either way, she would have to mail it from shore. She wasn't planning to go to Boston for a while.

Daisy made a scornful sound. "Who else could I mean? Of course Edward." She sighed. "I thought at one moment last night, when we went outside on the promenade for some air, that he would ask then. But he didn't."

Aria bit her lip, trying to hold back the words clamoring to get out. Despite Edward's obvious attributes and her efforts to be objective, she still didn't like him. Daisy would soon regret marrying him; she just knew it. "What are you wearing to the captain's dinner tonight?" she asked, changing the subject. Daisy had also received an invitation, as had Edward and Edith.

"I think I'll wear my Lucile." Daisy sat up straight. "You should wear yours too. It's the perfect occasion." She slid off the sofa and went to the call bell. "And we should have Turkish baths first. I'll make an appointment."

Daisy sent Molly off to inquire, and she soon returned. "There are two openings left, Miss Griffin. But you need to go right now."

"We'd better get ready, then," Daisy said.

Aria folded her letter and slid it into an envelope. She'd decided to make the lace a surprise. She could either mail it from New York or through the ship's post office. She hadn't decided.

The maid's eyes were wide. "Apparently the captain's dinner has everyone excited." She lowered her voice. "Mrs. Astor will be there too."

"At the dinner?" Daisy fished around the floor for her shoes.

Molly giggled. "I meant the baths, but I heard she and her husband are also attending the dinner. Her maid told me."

Daisy's eyes narrowed in interest. "Her maid? Do you socialize with all the servants?" She fastened her shoe buckles and stood.

"All the ones in first class. While the passengers are off having fun, we get together for meals, even a spot of music and dancing." Molly's white skin flushed red behind her freckles, and a little smile played about her lips.

Daisy pounced. "Is there someone special among the servants?" Her tone was sly, wheedling.

Molly blushed even darker. "Not really, miss. But I do admire Mr. Astor's gentleman. Patrick is his name."

"I think I've seen him," Aria said. She remembered spotting

the Astors and their servant companions while boarding. "Is he exceedingly handsome?"

"Oh my, yes." Molly's hands twisted in her apron. "But that's not his only attraction. He can sing, and he's very nice too."

"I'll bet he is." Daisy piled two wool wraps in Molly's arms. "Be a love and follow us, will you? I think we might need these after."

Aria had never taken a Turkish bath, so she had no idea what to expect. The spa was suitably exotic, with green-and-blue-tiled walls and floors and gilded scrollwork. An attendant asked what they wanted. Daisy said the full treatment, so they were shown into changing rooms to disrobe. To Aria's relief, a long piece of cloth was provided for modesty, and she wrapped up like a Grecian maiden.

The attendant guided them through a series of rooms of varying temperatures—steamy, hot, temperate, and then cool. By the end, relaxing on a chaise with water and fruit, Aria felt like a limp rag and ready for a nap.

Daisy pawed at her blond, freshly washed mop. "I'm going to need someone to do my hair for dinner. It's a mess."

A young woman lying on a nearby chaise enjoying the *Titanic*'s novel treatment, a bed warmed by lightbulbs, turned her head. That was all that was visible since the bed was covered to keep in the light and heat. "I beg your pardon, but are you Miss Griffin?"

"Why yes, I am. To whom do I have the pleasure of speaking?" Then Daisy's mouth dropped open. "Mrs. Astor. How nice to see you."

Mrs. Astor laughed. "I'd shake your hand, but I'm rather confined right now. I'm a great fan of your films, Miss Griffin. I wanted you to know that."

Daisy practically vibrated with pleasure. "Thank you. I'm very pleased to hear that." She turned to Aria. "Mrs. Astor, this is my good friend and chief writer, Miss Aria Greco."

Aria and Mrs. Astor exchanged greetings.

The attendant hurried to Mrs. Astor's side. "Your time is up, madam. In your delicate condition, only a few minutes are allowed." She began to open the metal lid of the contraption.

Aria and Daisy averted their eyes as the attendant assisted Mrs. Astor into a robe. Through the draped cloth, it was very apparent that she was several months pregnant.

Mrs. Astor tightened the belt of her robe. "I heard what you said about your hair, Miss Griffin. If you like, I'll lend you my maid, Gertrude. She's a genius with the curling iron."

Shortly after their return, Gertrude came to the stateroom as promised, a slender slip of a young woman carrying a valise with her supplies. "Where shall I set up, ma'am?" she asked politely, her eyes darting around the parlor.

"How about in here?" Daisy said, leading her to the table and chairs near the fireplace. Another knock sounded on the door. "Can you please get that, Aria?"

Aria opened the door to find Olive, Lord Henry's wife, standing there.

"Good afternoon, Aria." Olive swanned into the room, removing her gloves as she went. "I hope you don't mind me popping in like this."

"Of course not. Please do come in." Aria shut the door behind her, shrugging behind Olive's back at Daisy, who subtly signaled with her brows that she was equally confused at Olive's appearance.

Daisy hid her confusion behind a wide smile. "How nice to see you, Olive." She gestured to an armchair. "Please do sit down. How are you liking the voyage so far?"

Olive yawned, covering her mouth. "Please forgive me. We were up very late last night. You know Henry and the gaming table." One brow rose in an arched expression.

Daisy nodded. "Edward is equally as bad."

"Who is going first, ma'am?" Gertrude had unpacked her valise, setting out combs, brushes, false hairpieces, hair doughnuts, pins, feathers, and jeweled hair ornaments. She plugged in an electric curling iron, a contraption that held the tongs inside to warm them.

"I will, if you don't mind, Aria."

"Of course not," Aria said. "I'm simple compared to you." Aria favored a simple topknot rather than the elaborate curls Daisy liked.

Daisy sat at the table, and Gertrude began to comb her long locks. "We're getting ready for the captain's dinner," she told Olive.

"Oh, we're invited too." Olive eyed Gertrude speculatively. "Can you also do my hair?" She pushed at her high-piled tresses. "I just need a going over with the curling iron."

"This is Mrs. Astor's maid," Daisy said quickly.

"I can do it, ma'am," Gertrude said. "I have time."

"That's excellent, thank you." Olive removed her suit jacket. "I'll just be careful getting dressed for dinner."

Daisy and Olive chatted about who they had seen on the boat, what they thought of the amenities. Then Olive got personal. "So you are in moving pictures, Daisy. Do you like it?"

"I do, very much. I started out as a stage actress, but I find film much more exciting and less boring. Instead of acting in one play for weeks or months, we film something and it's done."

"Mr. Astor's man wants to be a film star," Gertrude said. "He's always acting out scenes from the movies." She pulled the tongs out and tested their heat with a wet finger.

"You mean the delectable Patrick?" Olive asked. "Mr. Astor loaned him to Henry when we were staying with the Marlboroughs in Italy."

"Is he any good?" Daisy's posture straightened. She loved finding new talent for her films.

Before Gertrude could answer, there was another knock on the door. Molly, bringing fresh towels. "He's very good indeed, ma'am," Gertrude said as Molly put the towels in the bathroom.

"Let's see how good," Daisy said. "Molly, can you please go to the Astors' suite and see if Patrick is available for an audition?" She glanced up at Gertrude. "Mr. Astor won't be dressing yet, will he?"

Gertrude shook her head. "Not yet, Miss Griffin."

"Go then, Molly. Quickly. And, Aria, pull out the Western scenario. And the gun."

"The gun?" Olive's face was comically alarmed.

"It's not loaded." Daisy pulled at one long curl and let it bounce back into place. "You're doing a wonderful job, Gertrude."

Gertrude ducked her head in a nod. "Thank you, ma'am. You have lovely hair, if you don't mind me saying."

Aria caught a sour expression flashing across Olive's face. But when she spoke to Daisy, her tone was pleasant, even warm. "You certainly do have beautiful hair." She patted her own with a laugh. "In contrast to mine, which is woefully thin and lacks body."

"Don't worry, Lady Norwich. I know exactly what to do."

Gertrude's reassurances didn't appear to mollify Olive, who probably expected a denial. Bowing her head, she flicked angrily at a piece of lint on her skirt. Feeling the rising tension in the room, Aria was relieved when Molly knocked and came in, followed by Mr. Astor's valet, Patrick. Once again, Aria was struck by the man's perfect features. He certainly had the looks to be in movies.

"Good afternoon, ladies." Patrick gave a bow and smiled at each woman in turn. "I'm at your service." He clasped his hands behind his back and stood, waiting.

"I understand you want to be in films," Daisy said.

"Yes ma'am, I do. How did you—"

"Gertrude told me." Daisy held out a piece of paper, a page from the scenario. "There is a role for a sheriff in my new picture." She nodded at Aria. "Miss Greco is the writer."

Patrick darted his eyes toward Aria as he took the page. "Very good, ma'am. I'll just study this for a moment." He studied the scene with a frown of concentration, muttering under his breath. Then he put the paper down and stood tall. "I'm ready, ma'am."

Daisy pointed at the gun, sitting on a side table. "There's your prop. Use it."

The valet started, much as he might if confronted with a snake. "A firearm? Is it real or a dummy?"

"It's real," Aria said. "But I made sure earlier that it wasn't loaded."

Patrick hesitated, but once he picked it up and began to act out the scene, it was apparent to Aria that he was a natural. She'd seen plenty of would-be actors who weren't. He became the sheriff confronting the bank robbers, exuding calm authority and decisive action. At the end of the scene, he gently placed the gun back on the table. Unlike many amateurs, he didn't demand a response, merely waited calmly for the verdict.

Olive broke into applause. "Bravo. Very nice."

Patrick smiled thanks with a little bow but looked to Daisy.

"I agree," Daisy said. "You were wonderful. Perfect, in fact."

His shoulders slumped briefly in relief. "Thank you. Will you give me a referral to your studio?"

"I'll do more than that. I'll give you a role." Daisy handed Gertrude a hairpin. "But I'll probably be retiring when I marry." She gave the maid another pin. "Then Miss Greco will help you."

Olive made a strange sound, almost a grunt. She tried to cover it by clearing her throat. "Are you engaged, Daisy?" Her voice was thin, high-pitched.

Daisy gave a tiny headshake so she wouldn't disturb Gertrude's work. "Not yet. But I will be shortly." She smiled. "To Edward, of course."

"That is wonderful. I recommend marriage highly." Despite her words, Aria noticed Olive's hands were clasped so tightly the knuckles were white. What could be bothering her?

Daisy realized Patrick was still hovering. "Give Miss Greco your address and we'll be in touch." With effusive thanks, he obeyed and left, escorted to the door by the smitten Molly.

Gertrude thrust in the last pin, and Daisy picked up a hand mirror and examined the updo, patting the pinned curls. "This is beautiful, Gertrude. My hair has never looked so good." She pushed back from the table. "Why don't you go next, Olive? I'm sure Henry is waiting for you."

Olive glanced at the clock. "Actually, I've asked him to stop by." She gave Daisy a sly smile. "I know the two of you are old friends."

"We are indeed." Daisy moved aside to let Olive sit in her chair.

Lord Henry arrived when Gertrude was finishing up Olive's curls. "Perhaps I should come back later," he said, taking in the scene—Daisy and Aria in dressing robes, his wife having her hair done.

"Nonsense. You've seen worse backstage dozens of times." Daisy took his arm and gently tugged him into the stateroom. "Come have a cup of tea while you wait for Olive."

At Daisy's nod, Molly poured Lord Henry a cup, and he perched on the edge of a sofa. "Very nice suite," he said, his eyes roving the room while he sipped at his drink. Then his eyes practically bugged out. "Good grief, is that a gun next to the curling iron?"

"Gertrude uses it when her ladies refuse to cooperate," Daisy said flippantly. She wandered over to the table and picked it up. "I guess I'd better put this away." She carried it into the wardrobe room.

"It was for an audition today," Aria said. "It's not loaded."

Olive's back was to her husband so it was fortunate she couldn't witness the longing glances he gave Daisy when she sauntered back into view. *No wonder Olive is jealous*, Aria thought. He was still carrying a torch for the actress.

"How are things with you, Daisy?" he asked in a soft voice as she seated herself in a chair, careful not to muss her hair.

Daisy threw him a dazzling smile. "Everything is brilliant, as you Brits say. I'm having the time of my life." She picked up her cup of tea and sipped.

"With Edward, you mean?" Lord Henry focused on his cup as though it held the world's secrets.

"That's right." Daisy set her cup down, then stretched and yawned. "That man wears me out with all the dining and dancing we've been doing." She smiled. "I'm very, very happy."

Olive gave a little grunt, causing Gertrude to pause while wielding the iron. "I didn't burn you, did I, Lady Norwich?"

"No no. I'm fine." Olive made an impatient gesture. "I do need to get going."

"Of course, milady." Gertrude quickly finished the last few strands. "There you are." She set the iron in its holder.

"Thank you so much." Olive dug around in her reticule and withdrew several bills. She pressed them upon Gertrude despite her protests. "No, I insist. Buy yourself something pretty." She jumped to her feet. "Ready, dear?"

After the couple left, it was Aria's turn. Gertrude accepted a generous tip from Aria and Daisy as well, with a promise to come again any time they needed her. Molly helped Daisy and Aria dress for dinner, a process interrupted several times by deliveries from the ship's flower shop. Edward, Lord Henry, the captain, and other admirers sent bouquets and corsages in honor of the festive occasion of the captain's dinner.

Molly had departed for her own dinner when there was another delivery, a long box signifying roses. But when Aria opened the box, expecting to find gloriously fragrant red or white blooms, she found twelve dead roses, withered, curled, and blackened.

Corinna, Vermont
Present Day

"That doesn't look like Ian," Julie said.

"They're giving me a bad feeling," Marla said.

"Me too." Sofia didn't like the men's slow, deliberate, threatening movements. As they drew closer, she noticed they wore black leather jackets and had shaved heads. One was clean-shaven; the other had a goatee. As if to underscore Sofia's uneasiness, Fergus began to bark from inside the Parkers' cottage, a distant yip.

"Ian Marshall here?" the clean-shaven one asked.

"No, he isn't." Julie's voice shook slightly. She cleared her throat. "Who wants to know?"

The man ignored the question. "Isn't that his ride?" He pointed at Ian's car.

"It is, but he's not here." Julie turned her head slightly. "Go get the men," she whispered. "Quick."

Marla darted into the kitchen, obviously planning to reach the fire pit where Jim and Mark were via the house instead of the yard.

Sofia moved to stand beside Julie in a show of support. "He's really not here, guys," she said.

The man with the goatee took a step forward, a gesture laden with menace. "Where is he?"

"We don't know," Julie said. "Honest."

The two men looked at each other. "I think you're lying,"

Clean-Shaven said. "You're probably hiding him. What a wimp." He threw back his head and yelled, "Marshall! Get out here."

To Sofia's relief, she heard thudding footsteps, and Jim and Mark appeared in the circle of light.

"What's going on?" Mark asked in a deceptively reasonable voice. Sofia noticed he held a long stick by his side, casually as though he just happened to have it. Standing just behind him, Jim discreetly held his cell phone.

"We're looking for Ian Marshall," Clean-Shaven said. "And this babe claims he's not here."

Mark took a step forward. "That 'babe' is my wife. And no, he's not here." He cocked his head. "What do you want with him anyway?"

"None of your business, man," Goatee said. "It'd be best if you just gave me the information."

"And we told you, we don't know," Jim said. He held up his phone. "And I'm calling the police if you're not out of here in three seconds."

The men exchanged glances again and apparently made a decision. They moved toward their car, Clean-Shaven detouring to hammer on Ian's hood with one fist. Then they jumped into their car, backed up, and roared away.

Sofia and the others stood in stunned silence as the red taillights on the sedan dwindled and then disappeared, fading along with the roar of the engine.

"I'm worried." Julie flung herself into her husband's arms. "Ian must be in trouble if guys like that are looking for him."

Jim and Mark exchanged looks over Julie's bent head. "You're right," Mark said. "They're bad news."

"Did you notice there wasn't a front license plate? And the plate light was out in back, so I couldn't get the number."

"How convenient," Sofia said.

"It would be great if the police stopped them for that," Marla said. "But it seems some people get away with everything."

Julie pulled back from Mark's arms. "Speaking of police, should we call them?"

"I don't think we have anything to report, hon." Mark sounded regretful. "Two men are looking for Ian. He's not here. That's not much for them to work with."

"I guess you're right." Julie crossed her arms, frowning. "What a mess."

"I know one thing," Mark said. "We're locking the doors tonight. And I suggest you do the same. It used to be safe down here, but now I don't know."

What a roller-coaster day, Sofia reflected as she and Jim walked back to their cottage a few minutes later. It started off badly with Ian's disappearance, was fun in the middle, and then ended with a visit from two unsavory characters. Were they on vacation, or had they stumbled onto the set of a thriller movie? She hoped tomorrow would be better.

The soft breezes off the lake and the scent of pine trees were lulling, and Sofia enjoyed a surprisingly good night's sleep. In the morning, she made pancakes and bacon with real Vermont maple syrup for the family, then wandered over to Julie's with a mug of coffee. It was another sparkling, blue-sky summer day, and a few boats were already around on the lake.

Julie and Marla were lounging in the wicker chairs on the big porch with their own cups of coffee. "Morning," Julie called as Sofia approached. "What's on the agenda for today?"

Sofia entered through the screen door, letting it slam behind her with a *thwack*. That sound always reminded her of summer. "Jim is going fishing along the shore with Mark and the boys. The girls are giving each other manicures and pedicures. So I think I'd like to go up to town and check out the antique store."

"That's a great idea," Marla said. "I'd like to find a farm stand and buy some local produce."

"There's one we always go to," Julie said. "They have the sweetest corn I've ever eaten."

"Yum. Corn on the cob, grilled in the husk." One of Sofia's favorite summer dishes. "Perfect with ribs, which I brought."

"Sounds perfect." Julie got to her feet with a groan. "But before we go anywhere, I'm having another cup of coffee. Anyone else want a refill?"

A short while later, the trio hopped into Julie's SUV and headed into the quaint village of Corinna. They found a parking space along the main road and walked the short distance to the antique store. Sofia gazed at the neat white houses they passed, enjoying the riotous flower gardens and window boxes and tubs overflowing with blooms. The sound of a lawn mower hummed, and the scent of cut grass hung in the air. Small-town summer perfection.

The antique store was housed in a two-story building with plate-glass windows. A former pharmacy, judging by the ancient Carter's Little Liver Pills sign high up on one side. There wasn't a porch, but pillars supported an upper balcony, and a set of outside stairs led up there. There were probably apartments or offices above the store.

Julie pressed the latch of the right side of the double door and pulled, causing bells to jingle. The store was one big room crammed with a jumble of furniture and items resting on every available surface. Along one wall was a set of built-in cabinets left over from the pharmacy days. The other walls held paintings and shelving. The overriding odor was the smell of dust and old wood with a hint of furniture polish.

"I love places like this," Marla said. "You never know what treasure you might find."

"Me too," Sofia said.

Near the back, she spotted a display case holding model ships. Maybe that was where they housed the marine collection. She pointed. "I'm going back that way."

Her friends followed, their footsteps thumping on the creaky, wide-board floor. A thin young woman with sleek, black hair and elfin features popped out of the back room, coffee mug in hand. "Let me know if I can help you."

"Are you Lea Jacobs?" Sofia asked.

The woman narrowed hazel eyes. "Yes, I am. Do I know you?"

Julie stepped forward. "The short answer is no, but you do know my brother, Ian Marshall."

"Oh, Ian." Lea flipped her hair back over her shoulder. "You must be Julie. He talks about you all the time. And those twin nieces of his." She flashed a tiny smile, displaying her dimples.

"Really?" Julie looked surprised. "Unfortunately, we don't see him very often."

Lea set her mug down on the glass-top counter and began to straighten some papers. "That's too bad." Sensing their eyes on her, she glanced up. "Is there anything in particular you're looking for today?"

Julie moved closer. "Actually, yes. I'm hoping you might know where Ian is."

Lea put one hand on her chest. "Me? I haven't seen him for days."

"He didn't stop by here the night before last?" Sofia asked.

The young woman shook her head, her brow creased. "No. What time was it? The store was probably closed."

"But you live upstairs, right?" Marla asked. "I heard your footsteps coming down."

Marla was right. Sofia had heard them as well.

Lea backed away from the counter, both hands up, looking

cornered. "What is this? So what if I was home? He didn't stop to see me, okay?"

"Lea, I'm sorry," Julie said. "It's just that I think he's in trouble." Her voice cracked on that last word, and her chin began to tremble.

Recognizing the signs of impending tears, Sofia spoke up. She quickly filled Lea in on Ian's arrival, his disappearance, and then the text to Ellie. Finally, she mentioned the men who had come to the cottage the previous night. "So you see, Lea, it doesn't add up to a pretty picture."

Lea's face had gone dead white, a sprinkling of freckles standing out on her upturned nose. She crossed her arms across her middle as though her belly hurt. After a long moment, she raised her head and gazed at them. "I don't know where he is, I swear. And I don't know anything about any trouble he's in, okay?" Her expression and firm tone said, *Don't ask me again.*

Julie's mouth opened, but Sofia put a detaining hand on her arm. "We understand, Lea. We certainly didn't come in here to drag you into Ian's problems." Sofia took a deep breath, attempting a laugh. "Actually, I'm hoping you know something about Etta Bannister."

Lea flipped her hair back again, smoothing it with one hand. "Oh, Etta. Sure. Her daughter, Clara, lives nearby. I've heard her lecture at the historical society meetings about her mother's experience on the *Titanic*."

"Do you think she would be willing to talk to me? I just found out that I have a relative who was on the *Titanic* too. Aria Greco. She was a writer."

"And she was traveling with a movie star," Julie said. "Daisy Griffin."

"Cool. I've heard of Daisy Griffin. We watched her silent

movies in my film class. As for Clara, I'm not sure. She hasn't been doing very well lately. Her granddaughter Amy stays with her these days. But you could always ask." She reached for a pen standing in a mug and scrawled notes on a piece of paper. "You probably have GPS, but even GPS can't find this place."

Julie studied the directions. "It must be out near the farm stand."

"That's right. Her house is down the road from there." Now that the subject of Ian was dropped, Lea appeared friendly, even eager to please. "We have some memorabilia from the *Titanic*, if you want to see it. Reproductions since most of the real stuff is still on the bottom of the ocean, of course."

"Sure, I'd love to," Sofia said.

Lea showed them to a case below the one holding model ships. In addition to compasses, spyglasses, and other marine items, there were a couple of small blue-and-white boxes. She slid open the rear door and retrieved one.

"There's a copy of a menu for the last dinner, tickets, luggage stickers . . ." Lea set each item out on the countertop. "Even deck plans of the ship."

"This is grim." Julie pointed to one piece. "The telegram about the iceberg."

Sofia read the message.

> *We have struck iceberg = sinking fast = come to our assistance = position: Lat 41.46 N. = Lon 50.14 W.*

"That is awful," Lea said. "To think they were having the time of their lives while heading for disaster."

Kind of like Ian, Sofia thought. *Though you might say the same for anyone.* Unfortunately, tragedies and trouble didn't often announce themselves in advance.

Sofia turned to Lea. "I'll take it."

"This must be Clara's house." Julie slowed the SUV in front of a rambling farmhouse with a red barn that was set back from the road in a gently sloping field. Rolls of hay sat here and there, gathered into the form that always reminded Sofia of giant servings of shredded wheat.

Her stomach tightened with anticipation as Julie turned up the gravel drive. "I hope she's willing to see us."

"Me too," Marla said. "She's the nearest thing to an eyewitness we have, next to those written accounts."

Julie pulled to a stop next to a Subaru wagon and a pickup truck. "Looks like someone is home."

They piled out and trooped to the back door, set inside a small, windowed porch. Sofia rapped on the back door, but her view through the door glass was blocked by a café curtain. A small dog yipped inside, and she heard footsteps, along with the admonishment to be quiet.

A woman in her thirties pulled back the curtain and peered out, then opened the door. Her long hair was piled up in a messy topknot, and she wore an apron over a pair of jeans and a T-shirt. On the stove behind her, a large pressure canner steamed.

"Sorry, I'm in the middle of canning green beans." She pushed at her damp forehead with one forearm. "Can I help you?"

Sofia introduced herself and her friends, and the woman introduced herself as Amy.

"I had a relative who was a *Titanic* survivor," Sofia said, "and Lea at the antique shop said your grandmother often gives lectures about it. We were hoping we could speak to her."

"Not today. She's napping. Come back in the early morning;

that's when she's at her best." Amy gave them a rueful smile. "She just turned ninety. You know how it is."

Sofia's heart sank. She didn't want to bother someone who was apparently failing. "Only if it's all right with her—and you."

"Oh, it will be fine. She loves nothing more than to talk about the *Titanic*." She smiled again. "It's all she talks about some days." She patted her apron pockets and pulled out a pencil. "Let's exchange numbers. Give us a call before coming over."

Sofia sighed in disappointment as they drove away. "I hope we'll get a chance to talk to Clara. I feel like she's our only living link to Aria."

"The last survivor died in 2009," Marla said, "and she was an infant in 1912. So you're right, Clara is the next best thing."

Julie signaled and turned into another farmyard. "Here we are. This is the farm stand."

Rather than an actual stand outside, the farm sold produce inside one of the barns. They joined other customers browsing the tables and bins, selecting produce and weighing it.

"We're in luck. The Silver Queen is in." Julie held up an ear of corn in triumph. She began to pull back the husks enough to check the kernels, putting the best ears into a paper sack.

"Picked fresh this morning," the attendant said. He patted his chest, clad in a Grateful Dead T-shirt. "By me."

Marla, meanwhile, was picking over a tray of ripe tomatoes. "These are gorgeous." She carefully set half a dozen inside a sack.

"Aren't they?" Sofia selected a pint of yellow cherry tomatoes and ten baby zucchinis. She could cut them in half, sprinkle them with herbs, and grill them. Even Matthew had been known to eat one.

At the table, Sofia asked the attendant, "Is this your farm?"

He shook his head as he punched keys on an old-fashioned adding machine. "No ma'am, it belongs to my cousins. I come down from Burlington on Saturdays to help." He flashed a grin. "I get to take produce home as part of my pay."

"Yeah, we have to rein Jason in," another young man said. "He loves his veggies."

"Consider it a marketing expense, Travis. I tell all my foodie friends all about you guys."

"It's working," Julie said, plunking her load on the counter. "This place is packed."

A few minutes later, they loaded their purchases in the SUV and headed for home.

"Want to get out the paints this afternoon?" Sofia asked. "I'm itching to do a view of the lake."

"That sounds good." Marla flapped the neck of her T-shirt. "But I might take a dip first. It's getting steamy." The time was close to noon, and along with the increased intensity of the sun, the humidity was also rising.

"Yes, it's going to be a scorcher," Julie said. "The weather forecast says temps are going to be close to ninety over the next few days."

"Perfect vacation weather." Sofia's spirits lifted as they wound their way onto the now-familiar lake road. How wonderful to spend the dog days of August on the water—and in it.

They bumped and jolted down the drive to the rear of Julie's cottage. The first thing Sofia noticed was that Ian's car was still there. Then she saw the navy-blue sedan parked to the far side of the area.

"Do you know who that is?" Sofia asked Julie.

Julie shook her head, frowning. "No. I sure hope it's not those men from last night."

"It doesn't look like the same car," Marla said. "For one thing, it's clean."

"True." Julie parked, and the trio scrambled out. As they did so, the doors of the other car opened, and a man and a woman stepped out. Both were wearing suits, an odd choice for a hot summer day, and sunglasses.

They were law enforcement. Sofia just knew it. Dread iced her core.

10

Titanic
April 12, 1912

Aria stared at the dead roses in horror. Who could have sent such a thing? She set the box on the table and searched for a card. There wasn't one.

To her dismay, she heard Daisy's footsteps. She hastily put the lid on the box, but in her nervousness she fumbled, sending the entire thing to the floor.

"What on earth are you doing?" Daisy's footsteps quickened. "Here, let me help." She crouched to pick up one of the flowers, then recoiled. "It's dead."

"They all are, Daisy. Someone sent you a dozen dead roses." Aria crammed the flowers back into the box.

Daisy put a hand on her arm. "Wait. Call the purser. Maybe he can find out who sent these."

"Good idea." Aria rang the bell with shaking fingers. The person who sent the roses must be the same person who wrote the threatening notes. There couldn't be two such unhinged and hateful persons, could there? But unlike at the hotel, where they had freedom of movement, now they were trapped on a ship for the next several days. What if the threats escalated further?

Molly answered, and Aria sent her for Mr. Pierce. "Tell him it's urgent."

Molly's face was a study in curiosity, but Aria blocked her

view of the room, and the stewardess reluctantly headed off to find him.

Two raps on the door announced Mr. Pierce. "What's wrong, Miss Greco?" he asked when she let him in. "I don't mind saying I was concerned by Molly's message."

"What did she say?" Aria led him to the table, where the box of crumpled flowers lay.

"Something about a matter of life and death." His gaze fell on the roses. "Oh, is that it? The flowers need to be changed out?"

Aria held up a blackened rose, the bloom drooping. "I'll say. These arrived like this just a few moments ago."

Confusion followed by concern flashed across his face. "That's entirely unacceptable. I'll have a word with the florist."

"No, Mr. Pierce. It's not the florist's fault. These roses were sent to Daisy like this on purpose." She pushed back the tissue in the box, showing him the rest of the dozen. "One dozen dead roses."

Daisy emerged from her room. "That's right, Mr. Pierce. I've gotten some nasty notes too. This is just another incident in the same vein."

Mr. Pierce drew himself up, eyes flashing. "You received nasty notes on board the *Titanic*? That's appalling."

"No, she got them in Monte Carlo," Aria said. "But that means the same person is now on board. We have no idea who it is but thought you could speak to the steward who brought them and see what he knows."

"I'll do that." Mr. Pierce gathered up the box. "I'll take this with me and ask around."

That evening, the captain's dinner was held in the à la carte restaurant in one of the alcoves at the back of the room. As Aria drew closer, she saw Lord Henry, Olive, Edward, Edith, and Lord and Lady Duff-Gordon seated with the captain. To her surprise, she also saw Mr. Pierce at the table.

The men rose as Daisy and Aria approached, and introductions were made. The captain hadn't met Daisy, and neither Daisy nor Aria had officially met the Duff-Gordons.

"I recognize that dress," Lady Duff-Gordon said. "It's one of mine."

Daisy twirled around to display the white dress with its black velvet bow. "It certainly is. And I love it."

"I'm so glad," Lady Duff-Gordon said. "It looks exquisite on you."

Aria wished she had worn her own Lucile dress, but at the last moment, she had worn an old standby. Daisy was bewildered. She didn't understand Aria's odd habit of saving something new rather than wearing it immediately. Aria didn't understand it herself, except that her mother always warned her to be careful of her clothes, and she apparently took that to extremes.

"Please be seated," Captain Smith said.

Daisy was placed beside him, the seat of honor, and Aria beside Mr. Pierce, something she didn't mind in the least.

"We'll begin in a minute," the captain said. "We're waiting for two more guests." The waiter bent to speak in his ear, and the captain rose again. "Here they are."

Aria turned her head to see a pleasant-faced woman headed their way, in the company of Pierre Lafitte. She glanced at Daisy, whose face had gone white with shock. Then she recovered with a smile that only someone who knew her well would recognize as false. But Aria noticed that she refused to look Pierre in the face.

"I'd like to present Mrs. Margaret Brown," the captain said, "and Monsieur Pierre Lafitte." He went around and introduced everyone, and they all sat again.

Mrs. Brown immediately got the table laughing with a hilarious yet tasteful description of her experience at the Turkish bath.

"Fancy meeting you here," Aria said behind her hand to Mr. Pierce as the waiter placed bowls of consommé in front of them.

"Dining at the captain's table is part of my duties." He picked up his spoon. "Some evenings it is more pleasurable than others."

"I hope tonight is one of them." Amazed at her own bold words, Aria looked away, feeling her face burn.

Mr. Pierce leaned close. "It certainly is, with your delightful company, if I may be so bold as to say such a thing."

"I'm flattered, sir." Aria took a quick sip of soup, almost choking in her haste. Why couldn't she be like Daisy, who was charming the captain and Lord Duff-Gordon? Glancing around the table, she saw that Lord Henry, Edward, and Pierre were all watching Daisy. Olive's expression darkened at her husband's interest in the actress, and Edith made a show of turning to Mrs. Brown and starting a who-do-you-know conversation.

"Tell me more about your work, Miss Greco. How do you develop ideas?" Mr. Pierce appeared genuinely interested.

"I have lots of ideas, too many to develop. So I choose the most promising ones—or what I think are promising—and run them by Daisy. Other times, a director or producer will want a certain scenario, so I write that."

"I can tell you really enjoy your work," Mr. Pierce said.

"I do." She bit her lip, thinking of the uncertainty she struggled with constantly. Despite her success writing for Daisy, future commissions were not assured, especially if the actress retired.

Mr. Pierce lowered his voice. "What is it, Aria?"

She shook her head. "Not a topic for the dinner table, I'm afraid." Glancing across the table, her eyes met Pierre's. He gave her a tiny salute with his wineglass, a gesture that made her belly tighten with anxiety. She hadn't even broached the topic of Pierre's overtures with Daisy, an omission that plagued her with guilt.

Over fillet of sole and roast beef, the conversation became general, with the captain expounding at length upon the magnificent ship's abilities. Aria noted gratefully that Lord Henry and Edward appeared to have put their differences aside, at least while dining with the captain. After the dessert and cheese courses, the assembly rose with groans, the men bound for the smoking room while the ladies adjourned for cards in the lounge.

Outside the restaurant, Daisy took Aria aside. "Let's go back to the stateroom. I really can't face another hour or two with the hens, although that Mrs. Brown is amusing."

Aria welcomed Daisy's suggestion. "That's fine with me. I don't like playing cards anyway."

They made their excuses and slipped down the corridor to the Grand Staircase. As they climbed the flight to their deck, Aria asked, "I'm surprised you're not spending more time with Edward tonight."

"Oh, but I am. We're taking a walk on the deck later." Daisy grabbed Aria and began to dance around in circles. "This could be the night!"

Oh, how Aria hoped not, for both their sakes.

In the stateroom, Daisy curled up with a book, and Aria sat down with the Western scenario. As she worked on the scenes, she found herself imagining the valet Patrick in the starring role.

"Patrick was really good, wasn't he?" Aria asked.

Daisy marked her place with a finger. "Yes, he was. I wasn't expecting that. So many times people want to audition and they're just terrible." She cocked her head, silent for a minute. "But he had something extra—a certain depth."

A gentle knock sounded on the door, and Daisy jumped. "Maybe that's Edward." She put down her book and began to pat at her hair. "Can you please answer? I'm a fright." She slid off the sofa and dashed for her bedroom.

Aria reluctantly opened the door, forcing herself to smile a greeting. But to her surprise, it was Pierre Lafitte standing there.

"I'm sorry to bother you so late, mademoiselle, but may I have a word with you?"

"That's really not such a good idea right now." Aria glanced back over her shoulder, hoping she could get rid of him before Daisy discovered their guest's identity.

"I'll only take a minute of your time, I promise." His smile was an attempt to be charming. Was she going to be forced to close the door in his face?

"Let him in," Daisy called. "I'll be right out."

Pierre's grin widened. "You heard the lady." Using his broad shoulder, he pushed his way into the room.

Aria lowered her voice to a fierce whisper. "You'd better leave, or I'll call the purser."

Pierre widened his stance, standing firm on stocky legs. "You disappoint me, mademoiselle. I thought we were becoming friends."

Footsteps thudded against the carpet. "I was wondering—" Daisy stopped in her tracks. "What are you doing here, Pierre?"

He bowed slightly. "I have come on a matter of business with Mademoiselle Greco. But I would be happy to include you in our discussion, Daisy." His use of her first name underscored their formerly close relationship.

"How dare you?" Daisy shrieked through gritted teeth, stamping one foot. "I want nothing to do with you. Get out!" She pointed toward the doorway, her hand shaking.

He didn't move. "Can we not talk about this? Surely this show of temper is a trifle excessive."

In response, Daisy clenched her fist and stamped her foot on the carpet. "Go, before I have you removed. I despise you. Everything you have done is despicable."

"What have I done?" He sounded genuinely puzzled.

"Threatening me, for one." Daisy drew herself up to her full height. "It's no good. Whatever you say I will deny."

Realization dawned in Aria's mind. Daisy believed Pierre was responsible for the notes and the roses. *The truth will come out.* What had Daisy done?

"I think you should go," Aria said to Pierre.

He sighed deeply. "I suppose you are right. Good night, ladies." The door closed behind him.

Daisy whirled on Aria. "Explain something. What is the business he wanted to discuss with you?" Bright spots of color stood out against her pale complexion. Her voice shook. "How could you go behind my back this way, Aria?"

Aria sank down onto the sofa, ill with guilt and remorse. If only she had told Daisy everything about her encounters with Pierre earlier. Now it was as though their friendship hung in the balance. Words, usually tools in her deft hands, jumbled in her mind like nonsense. What should she say? What could she say?

Finally, she took a deep breath and opted for the simple truth. In as few sentences as possible, she told Daisy the substance of their conversation on the train and on the *Titanic*. "I didn't intend to betray you, Daisy. But frankly, I don't understand your aversion to the man and your decision to break your contract." Self-righteous anger surged, and Aria jumped to her feet. "We've been getting legal notices from Pan-Francais, something you've ignored, leaving the worry in my lap. That's not fair."

Daisy considered this as she paced back and forth in front of the fireplace. "I suppose you're right on that point. I've been hoping the whole thing would just go away."

Aria's anger fled at her friend's acknowledgment of her concern. "There's another thing. You've been talking about marrying Edward. But if you do, what is to become of me? I have to think about my career, and Pierre wants to hire me."

Daisy didn't respond as she stopped to stare moodily into the gas fire.

Aria pressed on. “And I don’t understand why you are so dead set on marrying Edward. Do you really love him? I can’t believe it.” She took a deep breath, knowing that her next words might tear them apart irrevocably. However, she couldn’t stand by and watch her best friend make a terrible mistake. “Daisy, he treats you like just another possession. He’s not like Lord Henry, who I believe really—”

“How *dare* you.” Daisy raised her head and glared at Aria. Her voice was low and furious. “Edward loves me.” She waved one arm wildly. “You wouldn’t know. You’ve never been in love.”

Her words hit Aria like a blow. It was true. She hadn’t been in love or had someone love her. She had always been the somewhat plain girl in the background, shadowed by Daisy’s brilliance.

“You’re right, Daisy. I haven’t.” Aria walked on trembling legs toward her room. “Do what you want. I wish you well.”

“Aria!” Daisy’s voice was a plaintive cry. When Aria didn’t answer, she called out, “I’m going to see Edward. And I’m not coming back until he asks me to marry him.” With that final word, she slammed out of the stateroom.

Aria collapsed onto her bed, feeling as battered as if she had been thrown off a horse. She replayed the scene over and over in her mind until she couldn’t stand it anymore. She needed fresh air and lots of it.

Throwing on a cloak, she went up the back staircase to the deck. She didn’t want to see anyone she knew and have to engage in social pleasantries. Out on deck, a cold wind swept down around the funnels and blew along the length of the ship. She tucked her head down and stalked forward, hoping the brisk exercise would clear her head.

Aria’s steps faltered. A lone man stood at the very tip of the bow. Whoever it was must have sensed her presence because he turned.

Mr. Pierce.

Aria stood, irresolute. Should she turn around and go back, or would that be intolerably rude?

He relieved her of the decision. With a wave, he strode toward her. "Cold night, isn't it? You can tell we're getting into Artic waters."

She put both hands over her frozen ears. "You're right."

"Here." He unwound the muffler draped over his coat and handed it to her.

"Are you sure?" At his nod, Aria wrapped the soft wool around her head and neck. It had a faint piney scent Aria had noticed on Mr. Pierce himself. "Thank you."

He held out his arm to her, guiding her on a circuit of the deck. She was thankful that he didn't press her into conversation as they strolled along, gazing at the dark, glassy ocean and the glitter of stars.

"We're moving at top speed," he said when they paused in a sheltered area to stare overboard. Far below, water churned against the hull as the ship pressed forward.

Aria picked up a note of concern in his tone. "Is that a problem?"

He shook his head, annoyed. "I'm sorry, I shouldn't have said that. I'll be sacked if the captain learns I've been discussing the ship's performance with the passengers."

"What do you mean? He was bragging about the speed himself." When he remained silent, she said, "Tell me. I promise I won't say a word to anyone."

Mr. Pierce looked both ways before leaning close and whispering in her ear. "I don't have a good feeling about our route combined with our speed. This ship is far too large to turn aside quickly if we should come across an obstacle."

"An obstacle?" Aria had no idea what he meant.

"Ice," was his succinct reply. He held out his arm again. "Come on, let's get you below. You must be freezing."

True, her toes were starting to tingle and her fingers were numb, but Aria didn't want to leave Mr. Pierce's side. She walked as slowly as possible back to the doorway and down the stairs to her level.

"Do you have your key?" he asked outside her stateroom door. She handed it to him, and he unlocked the door and pushed it wide. "There you go."

"Would you like to come in for a cup of tea?" Aria unwound his scarf and handed it to him.

Mr. Pierce cocked his head, a pleased smile flitting across his lips. "Are you sure? It's getting late."

"Absolutely." She rubbed her hands together. "It will help warm us up." Aria entered the stateroom, followed by the purser. "Let me ring for a steward."

Before Aria could ring the bell, thudding footsteps sounded in the hallway. Someone rattled the doorknob and then, seeing it was open, burst in.

"I'm so glad you're here, Mr. Pierce." A hand to her chest, Daisy panted, trying to regain her breath. "Edward is dead."

11

Corinna, Vermont
Present Day

The strangers turned and waited for them to approach. Then the man flashed a badge. "Julie Butler? Agent Rico, Federal Bureau of Investigation."

"FBI?" Julie echoed. "What are you doing here?" She sounded stunned, a feeling Sofia could relate to.

Rico glanced at the other agent. "Agent Barnes and I are here to talk to Ian Marshall."

"He's not here," Sofia said. "We don't know where he is."

"Isn't that his vehicle?" Rico asked.

"It is," Julie said, "but my brother isn't here. Honest."

Agent Barnes sighed. "Can we go inside and talk?"

Julie started, remembering her manners. "Of course. Just let me grab some of my groceries from the car." She opened the SUV's hatch and grabbed a couple of produce bags. Sofia and Marla stepped up to do the same. Once inside, Julie dumped her bags on the kitchen counter, followed by Sofia and Marla.

Julie clasped her shaking hands in front of her waist. "Would you like coffee?" she asked the agents as Marla walked back to the door to retrieve the package that had been delivered that afternoon—the Daisy Griffin movies they'd ordered, no doubt.

"Something cold would be nice." Rico pulled back a kitchen chair without invitation, joined by Barnes.

Marla jerked open the refrigerator door. "We have iced tea."

"That's fine," Barnes said. "I appreciate it. It's a hot one out there."

Sofia grabbed glasses from the cupboard while Marla retrieved the pitcher from the fridge and ice trays from the freezer.

"We were supposed to meet Ian here yesterday, but we were held up." Rico nodded his thanks when Sofia placed a glass in front of him.

Julie took a seat and wrapped her arms around herself. "Why were you going to meet him? Is he in trouble?" She bit her lip, obviously dreading the answer.

The two agents eyed each other before Rico responded, "No, he's not in trouble, but he is wanted as a witness."

"To what?" Julie began to pace. "What's this all about?"

The agents stared at each other again before Barnes spoke. "First, tell us where he is."

Sofia and Marla began unpacking the groceries while Julie walked the agents through the sequence of events, how Ian had come to the cottage unexpectedly and then disappeared the next morning and how the thugs had tried to strongarm information about Ian from the women. "You can ask the local police if you doubt us. They spent some time on the lake looking for him."

Barnes made a note, confirming the times of Ian's arrival and when they had noticed him missing.

Marla took up the story as she pulled tomatoes and corn from their bags and placed them on the counter. "We think he might have taken the neighbor's kayak. He said it was missing. But we have no idea where he is."

"He could be in Canada by now," Julie said. "Please, tell us what's going on."

"All right," Rico said. "But this can't leave this room. Ian reported some suspicious activity going on in his place of employment and contacted us."

"The property management company?" Sofia asked.

"That's right," Rico said. "It's essential that we find him. He claims to have information that supports his allegations, and that is crucial to our investigation."

"You're welcome to look through his car and the belongings he left here," Julie said.

"We'll do that," Barnes said. "But there's something else. We want to find Ian for his own protection. These are very dangerous folks he's been messing with. His life could be in danger."

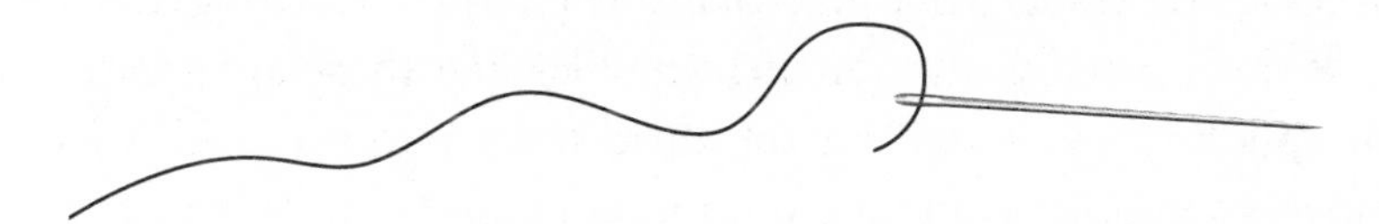

That evening, when their dinner of barbecued ribs and corn on the cob was over, the adults sat on the screened porch, enjoying coffee and dessert while the kids played a game of kick the can, running and calling out in the twilight. The women shared with their husbands what had occurred earlier that day.

"So that's all they said?" Mark asked. "Ian's life could be in danger?"

"That's it." Julie snuggled closer to her husband. "They wouldn't give us more details."

"What did they say about those thugs who came to pay a visit?" Jim asked.

"Not much," Sofia said. "But they did pump us for as much description as we could remember."

"Well, let's hope they don't pay a return visit," Mark said. "Did the agents leave a number?"

"They certainly did. They told us to call immediately if we hear from or see Ian." Julie drank the final sips of her decaf coffee. "I'm ready to relax. Let's watch the Daisy Griffin movies tonight."

"I think I'll take a rain check," Jim said. "I want to figure out where we're going fishing tomorrow. I heard there are landlocked salmon out there."

Mark grinned. "There are. And I know exactly where they hide."

The women left Jim and Mark to their fishing stories and headed over to Sofia's cottage to watch the movies in peace.

Sofia's living room was cozy, with comfy chintz-covered furniture. After she prepared a big bowl of popcorn and fetched everyone a soft drink, they settled in to watch Daisy Griffin's films. Sofia and Marla shared the sofa while Julie sat in an upholstered rocking chair.

"I don't usually care for silent movies, but these are great," Julie said as they waited for the third feature to start. All the segments were short, about ten minutes long.

Sofia picked up the DVD case and pulled out the liner, which had notes about the actors and crew. She gasped. "This next one was written by A. Greco. Aria was a screenwriter!"

"Fabulous," Marla said. "I've heard that many early movies were written by women."

The opening scenes of *A Lady in Paris* flickered, and they enjoyed watching the story of a young American visiting Paris who is both shocked and amused by the Parisians. At the end, Daisy joined a line of cancan girls, and they kicked and danced offstage, one after the other.

"That was great." Marla winked at Sofia. "Very well-written."

Sofia laughed. "I was going to say that, but I didn't want to brag about my relative."

"Consider me a fan." Julie passed the popcorn bowl back to Marla. "How many more are there on this DVD?"

"Three more," Sofia said. "Want to save them for another night?"

"Sure," Marla said. "Why gobble them all up at once?"

Julie seemed distracted, and Sofia noticed her staring off into space. "What is it, Julie?"

"I'm sorry," her friend said. "I'm having trouble getting Ian's situation out of my mind."

Sofia got up and gave her a supportive hug. "I don't blame you. I'd feel the same way if it were my brother."

"I want to go back to that antique store tomorrow," Julie said. "I think Lea knows more than she's letting on."

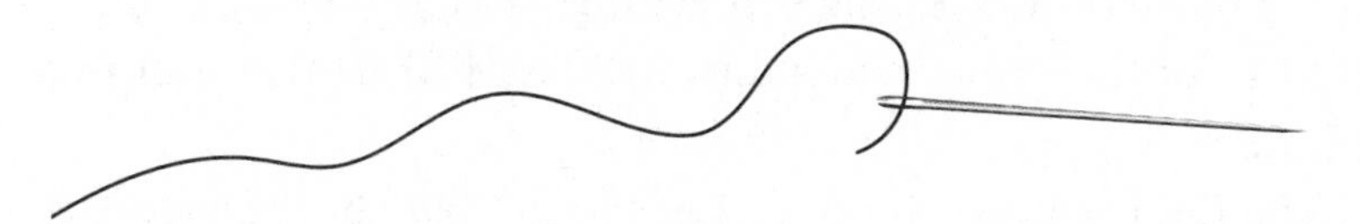

The next morning, Vanessa, Wynter, and the twins went to Burlington to shop while the boys and Fergus went out in the pontoon boat with Jim and Mark to do some fishing. Sofia and the other Pinot Painters drove into the village.

Once again, Main Street was fairly quiet, but the store's Open sign was turned the right way.

"I hope Lea is working today," Julie said as she pulled into a parking space across from the shop.

Sofia slid out of the passenger seat and waited for the other two to join her. A couple of cars passed, and they crossed the street.

The antique store appeared deserted, but Sofia heard sounds in the back room. Sure enough, as they approached the counter, Lea popped out, holding a mug. The anticipatory smile on her face vanished when she saw who it was.

"Oh, hi." Lea leaned against the doorjamb and took a sip. "How can I help you today?"

Sofia stepped forward. "Thanks for giving us Clara's address. We're going to go back sometime in the next few days to talk to her."

"Cool." Lea shrugged, as if to say *So what?* She scanned each face. "Is there anything else you need?"

"Actually, yes." Julie moved to the counter. "I really need to find my brother."

Lea straightened, annoyance flashing across her face. "I told you, I don't know where he is." She held up one hand. "I swear. Asking me again won't change that."

Sofia noticed Lea fidgeting, wiggling her knees back and forth. The clerk was hiding something. "It's urgent, Lea, or we wouldn't bother you." She paused. "The FBI is also looking for Ian."

The mug almost fell out of Lea's hand, but she managed to hold on to it. "Are you serious? The FBI?" The freckles across her nose stood out against dead-white skin.

"Yes, the FBI," Julie said angrily. "Imagine my reaction when two agents showed up at my cottage. This is serious stuff."

The clerk set her mug on the glass countertop with a *clunk*, covering her mouth with her freed hand. She shook her head, fear and confusion in her eyes.

"Let us help," Marla said. "You're in over your head, aren't you?"

Lea blinked furiously, on the verge of tears. "You're right," she whispered. "I am."

A car squealed to a stop in front of the shop. Sofia and the others turned to look. A dark sedan, similar to the one their night visitors used. Car doors slammed, and three men got out.

"Isn't that . . ." Julie's voice was a squawk.

"Yes it is," Sofia said.

The men moved toward the front door—slowly, and with an air of menace.

"Let's go." The women turned to see Lea gesturing frantically at them. "Those guys are dangerous." Turning, she darted through the doorway to the back room. Sofia and the others followed.

"Shouldn't we call the police?" Marla asked.

"No, they'll never get here in time."

Behind them, bells jingled and the front door slammed. Footsteps thumped.

Lea led them through a kitchen and into a back hallway. On either side were rooms filled with boxes and other inventory, and there was a door with a glass panel at the end. To the right was a staircase that obviously led to Lea's living quarters.

"This way." She turned the deadbolt lock and pulled the back door open. There was a narrow porch and a short flight of stairs heading down, since the building was set on a sloping lot.

"Where are we going?" Julie asked.

"Follow me." Lea sprinted across a swath of lumpy, overgrown grass, crossed a narrow lane with cracked asphalt, and entered the gates of a small cemetery. In the foreground, most of the gravestones were short and couldn't provide any cover, but at the rear stood a copse of pines and a couple of mausoleums. Lea wove through the grave sites in that direction, Sofia and the others panting along behind her.

Sofia's heart pounded, her feet as lead, feeling like she was in one of those slow-motion dreams being chased by bad guys. Her back tingled with the knowledge that she was a highly visible target, but she didn't dare glance over her shoulder to see if the men were in pursuit.

Upkeep apparently didn't extend to that corner of the cemetery, for the ground under the group of pines was thick with needles, leaves, and brush. Lea pushed through brambles at the rear of the closest structure, a square, squat building engraved with the name Bates.

Behind the building, Lea squatted behind the bushes. "Get down," she whispered, her voice almost a hiss. They obeyed, crouching so as not to touch the damp, cold ground.

"Can you see them?" Julie whispered.

"One of them is on the back porch," Lea whispered back. She craned her neck, watching.

So where are the other two? Sofia's heart beat even faster, making her head swim. She pictured the men figuring out where they were and coming to find them. Where could they go? Behind them lay thick, tangled woods. Could they run to another house? Not without crossing open land.

She started groping in her pocket, trying to take out her cell phone. "I'm going to call the police."

Lea shook her head. "Wait a minute. He's in the road looking around. He might hear you." She continued to watch, alert. "He went back inside." She rose to her feet, and Sofia and the others followed suit. Marla started to push through the brambles, but Lea stopped her. "Let's wait until we know they're really gone."

Hearing the roar of an engine, Sofia dared to peek around the corner of the mausoleum. She saw the sedan speeding away on the main road. "I'm still calling the police." She went for her phone again.

"Wait," Lea said. "What are you going to tell them? That some guys we didn't like came to the shop?"

Sofia paused. "True. But you know there's more to it than that."

Julie put her hands on her hips. "That's right, Lea. This situation confirms that you know more about Ian's problems than you've told us."

The young woman hung her head. "Yeah, I do." She dug into her jeans pocket and pulled out a flash drive. "Ian gave this to me before he disappeared."

Titanic
April 12, 1912

"I beg your pardon," Mr. Pierce said. "Did you just say that Edward is dead? Edward Thurston?"

"Yes." Daisy gave a wail and collapsed into Aria's arms. "It was awful, so awful."

Aria hugged Daisy tight, scarcely able to believe her ears. What could have happened to Edward? He had appeared to be in the best of health at dinner.

"Where is he?" Mr. Pierce asked.

"In his ca . . . ca . . . cabin," Daisy managed to get out between sobs. "On the rug."

"I need to go." Mr. Pierce bolted for the door. "Maybe he's still alive."

Aria disentangled herself from Daisy's arms. "I'm coming with you."

He halted, hand on the doorknob. "I'm not sure that's a good idea."

"Perhaps not." Aria gestured toward Daisy, huddled on the sofa. "But if it concerns Daisy, I need to know what is going on."

He seemed to accept this, and as they hurried through the door, Daisy called, "Wait for me. I'm coming too."

Edward's cabin was at the other end of the hallway, and the journey seemed endless to Aria. All those closed doors and acres of carpet, all identical, giving the impression that they never seemed to progress. Behind her, Daisy sniveled and sobbed, but Aria was thankful that she kept her voice down. All they needed was a curious crowd of onlookers.

The stateroom was unlocked. Mr. Pierce barged through, swiveling his head back and forth, searching for Edward. Then he grunted and ran for the far side of the room, crouching down beside the millionaire, who lay facedown near the bedroom door.

As Aria drew closer, she saw blood seeping out from under his body, soaking the carpet.

Mr. Pierce felt for a pulse on his neck anyway, then shook his head and stood. He turned a somber yet authoritative gaze on Daisy, who hovered just inside the stateroom door. "What happened, Miss Griffin? Were you here when he was killed?"

Daisy stared at him for a moment with wide blue eyes, not seeming to understand his words. Aria was ready to repeat the question when she said, "No. No, I wasn't." She took a step or two into the cabin. "When I knocked on the cabin door, he didn't answer. I noticed that the door was slightly open, so I poked my head in and called him." She sank back against the wall, shuddering, one hand to her mouth. "No answer, so I stepped inside. Then I saw him lying there."

"Did you touch him?"

"No. When I saw the blood, I knew he was gone."

"What time was that, Daisy?" Aria ran through the timing in her head. Daisy had left the cabin to find Edward about an hour ago. Where had she been all that time?

"Right before I came back to our stateroom, of course." Daisy's tone was bewildered.

"I must go," Mr. Pierce said. "I need to report this to the captain and the ship's doctor. Can I trust you two to wait here and not touch anything? They'll want to talk to you, Miss Griffin."

The door to the connecting cabin rattled, and Edith appeared in the doorway. "Edward?" She saw the trio standing there and halted, consternation on her face. "What are you doing in here?"

Mr. Pierce hurried toward her. "Mrs. Thurston, I have bad news for you." He attempted to guide her back into her cabin, but she obstinately pushed past him into Edward's parlor. She caught sight of the body and screamed.

"Edward! Edward!" She ran toward him.

Mr. Pierce put out an arm to hold her back. "Please, Mrs. Thurston, don't. I believe he has been shot."

Edith struggled in Mr. Pierce's restraining arms. "Shot? Who shot him?" She lunged toward Daisy. "Was it you? You . . . you pert piece of baggage." She writhed and twisted, snarling, intent on getting to Daisy, who shrank back in fear.

"Mrs. Thurston. Calm yourself." Mr. Pierce sent Aria a beseeching glance. "Can you please fetch the captain? One of the other officers can rouse the doctor."

"Of course." Aria fled the stateroom, grateful it wasn't her job to subdue Edith, who was understandably devastated by the loss of her son. She didn't know where the captain's cabin was located, so she headed for the bridge.

Only a couple of officers were on duty. Feeling the need to be discreet, she merely said it was an emergency and the captain and the ship's doctor were required. Fortunately, they didn't question her but promised to have the officers come to Edward's cabin right away.

As she hurried back to Edward's stateroom, she realized they could have rung for a steward. Mr. Pierce was obviously trying to minimize gossip, something she appreciated. Pausing outside the door, she hesitated, not wanting to go into the room again. But she supposed she had to support her friend and be available for questioning.

Inside, Daisy was huddled on a sofa, and Mr. Pierce was pacing.

"They'll be here soon."

"Thank you, Miss Greco. I'm going to take another look at the bedroom." Mr. Pierce stepped carefully around Edward's body and disappeared.

Aria glanced around. "Where is Edith?"

"In her stateroom, fortunately." Daisy blew her nose. "I can't believe the old battle-ax blames me for Edward's death."

"She has to blame someone," Aria said. "And you're handy." She took a deep breath and looked at the mantel clock. Twenty after eleven. "Daisy, you left our cabin around ten o'clock. But you didn't find Edward until, what, twenty minutes ago? I thought you were coming straight here."

Daisy flushed an angry red. "Are you accusing me of killing Edward too? This is a new low for you, Aria."

"No, I'm not. But if I'm asking, you know others will too."

As if in answer, a pounding knock sounded on the door. Aria opened it to discover Captain Smith, Dr. O'Loughlin, and Mr. Ismay, the managing director of the White Star Line. She had only seen Mr. Ismay from a distance but recognized him immediately.

"What's all this about an emergency?" Mr. Ismay's nose twitched.

Mr. Pierce emerged from Edward's bedroom. "Edward Thurston has been murdered."

His bald statement caused great consternation. Clutching his medical bag, the doctor rushed forward, followed by the captain.

"Murdered?" Ismay's face was bewildered. "Who on earth would want to do that?" He cast a suspicious glare toward Daisy and Aria.

"I have no idea," Mr. Pierce said.

"He's right. He was murdered," the doctor said, glancing up from his examination of the body. He and the captain had turned Edward over. Dr. O'Loughlin pulled open the bloody shirt, revealing Edward's chest. "He's been shot."

Aria turned away, not wanting to see anything else. Daisy put her hands over her eyes and began to cry again.

Ismay began to pace, wringing his hands. "This is a disaster, an absolute disaster. Everything is riding on this maiden voyage. A murder on board—"

"Unfortunately, murder is committed by a criminal." Captain Smith's tone was acerbic. "We need to find whoever it is before we arrive in New York and everyone disperses."

The adjoining stateroom door opened to reveal Edith. Her gaze scanned the room, landing in surprise on the ship's owner. "Mr. Ismay, thank goodness you're here. Are you going to find out who killed my son?" She pointed at Daisy. "Although you won't have far to look."

"What do you mean, madam?" Captain Smith drew himself up in dismay. "This isn't a woman's crime. Why are you blaming Miss Griffin?"

As everyone's eyes turned on Daisy, she gave a piteous whimper and touched her eyes with a hankie. Aria was sympathetic to her friend's distress but groaned inwardly when she recognized Daisy's act from a scenario they had recently filmed.

"Miss Griffin found Edward," Mr. Pierce explained. "I had just shown Miss Greco to their stateroom when Miss Griffin arrived with the news."

"What happened, Miss Griffin?" Captain Smith asked.

Daisy took them through the sequence of events, and then Aria and Mr. Pierce corroborated everything that had occurred after she came back to the stateroom.

"You didn't see anyone else leaving the cabin?" Captain Smith asked Daisy.

"No, I didn't. No one was in the hallway either."

Captain Smith turned to Edith. "Did you hear or see anything?"

"No, I'm afraid not. I was playing cards in the first-class lounge with Lady Duff-Gordon and Lady Olive until around eleven. The first thing I did when I got back was check on Edward." Edith grimaced. "I found Mr. Pierce and these ladies here instead."

"Death by person or persons unknown," Mr. Ismay said. "Perhaps it was a thief." He put a hand to his head. "The ship's reputation will be ruined."

"Worse, a young man has tragically lost his life." The doctor gave Mr. Ismay a forbidding glare. "I'll need to complete a more thorough examination, and then we'll need to ready him for burial at sea."

"No!" Edith screamed. "No. Don't throw him overboard. He must be buried in the family plot." She seized the captain's sleeve. "Tell the doctor he mustn't do that."

Captain Smith patted Edith gently on the shoulder. "Dr. O'Loughlin, we'll need to figure out where to hold Mr. Thurston's body, in deference to Mrs. Thurston's wishes."

The doctor nodded. "As you say, Captain. Call a couple of men, Mr. Pierce, and let's take him to the infirmary. I'll make my examination there."

"Wait." Mr. Ismay put up a hand. "I don't want this . . . disaster to become the subject of common gossip. As far as anyone needs to know, Mr. Thurston died of natural causes."

"Good grief, man." The captain was aghast. "We need to apprehend who killed him."

"And so we shall. But discreetly." Mr. Ismay's smile was cold. "Whoever he is, he can't have gone far, can he?"

Aria had to agree with Mr. Ismay. The person who had shot Edward was on board, no doubt of that. But where was the gun?

Mr. Pierce seemed to almost read her mind. "As you might

have noticed, gentlemen, the weapon is missing. I think we can safely assume it's lying at the bottom of the sea."

A short while later, Aria and Daisy left for their stateroom, hurrying along the silent hallway. Again, it seemed endless, and Aria longed for the sanctuary of her bed.

A door opened up ahead, and Aria braced herself. Who could be up at this hour?

Olive thrust her head around the half-open door. "What's going on? People have been going up and down the hall all night." Two stewards carrying a litter clattered down the back stairs and headed for Edward's cabin. After a knock, the door opened, and they slipped inside.

Lady Olive gasped. "Isn't that Edward's stateroom?"

Daisy didn't say anything, so Aria answered. "Yes, it is. Edward is . . . ill. They're taking him to the infirmary."

Olive sniffed. "That's too bad. He was drinking a lot tonight, Henry said. I guess it caught up with him."

"That must be it," Aria said. "Well, good night. See you in the morning."

Not waiting for a response, she took Daisy's arm and dragged her down the corridor, eager to get away before Olive asked any more questions. It wasn't going to be easy fending people off when they asked about Edward. Keeping the news of his murder quiet would require a miracle.

Daisy had passed her initial stage of grief and was practically comatose by the time they entered their stateroom. Aria helped Daisy undress like she was a large, inanimate doll, then tucked her into bed. As she reached to switch off the bedside lamp, Daisy spoke. "I loved him, you know."

Aria bit her lip, guilt at her dislike of Edward twisting in her belly. Now that he was gone, her opposition to their relationship seemed so petty. "I know, Daisy. I'm sorry for your loss."

Daisy turned on her side, drawing her knees up like a child curling into a ball. "He wasn't perfect, but he cared for me. I know he did, no matter what people said."

Aria leaned down and pulled the duvet up to cover Daisy's shoulders. On impulse she asked, "Where were you tonight, Daisy? After you left here and before you found Edward?"

Silence was her only answer. Aria went to the door and stood there for a moment before gently closing the door. A terrible idea had entered her mind the moment she heard Edward had been shot. Now, alone with her thoughts, fear and dread clutched her like a vise. She hurried to the wardrobe room and knelt in front of the trunk.

She dug through the clothing once, twice, three times. The gun and the bullets were gone.

13

Corinna, Vermont
Present Day

Lea handed the flash drive to Julie. "Ian told me"—she swallowed hard—"to keep this in case something happened to him."

Julie stared at the drive as though it were a poisonous snake. "This must contain the evidence the FBI was talking about."

"What kind of evidence?" Lea glanced over her shoulder, fidgeting. Sofia sensed that only politeness kept the clerk from bolting.

"We don't know," Sofia said. "But it's something to do with Ian's job."

Lea gave a tiny nod, as if that confirmed something she knew. "Listen, I'd better go lock the shop and grab some things. I'm going to get out of here before those guys come back." She began to stride across the grass.

"Where are you going to go?" Julie hurried to keep up with Lea. At Lea's headshake, she added, "In case we need to get ahold of you."

"I'll give you my cell number. But I'd rather not say where I'll be." She put her hand out to Sofia. "I'll put my number in your phone."

Sofia handed her phone over. Thumbs moving quickly, Lea entered her contact info and then passed it back. "Now I've got to get out of here. And I suggest you guys do the same."

"Wait a second, Lea," Julie said. "Do you know where Ian lives?"

Frowning in impatience, Lea rattled off a Burlington address. "His roomie is a guy named Jason."

"Does Jason work at the farm stand by chance?" Sofia remembered the young man who'd waited on her saying he lived in Burlington.

"That's right, he does." Lea pressed her lips together. "But that's all I know about him." She shuffled from foot to foot, obviously eager to leave. "Anything else?"

"Not right now, Lea," Julie said. "We'll let you know when Ian shows up. And if you see him first, please call me."

"I will. Take care," Lea called over her shoulder as she bolted across the cemetery.

A few minutes later, Sofia and her friends were in the sanctuary of the SUV, on the way back to the cabin. Sofia found herself watching every passing car, hoping not to see the threatening men again.

"I can't wait to get rid of this flash drive," Julie said. "It's burning a hole in my pocket. And I left Agent Rico's card at the cottage, so I have to wait to call him."

"We'll be there in a few minutes," Marla said. She reached over and patted Julie's knee. "Once they come get that thing, we're breaking out the paints."

"That's a great idea, Marla," Sofia said. "Nothing else relaxes me more."

They pulled into the parking area behind the cottage, and Julie jumped out as soon as she switched off the engine. Inside, Marla and Sofia made a fresh pot of coffee and set out muffins while Julie made the call in the other room. They could hear the urgency in their friend's voice as she relayed the morning's events.

"They'll be right over." Julie placed her cell phone and the flash drive on the kitchen table. "Fresh coffee. Just what I need." She sat down and doctored the mug Marla handed to her. "You two are the best."

"We'll do anything we can," Sofia said. "You know that, Julie."

"I'm just glad you're here. I'm not going to be able to relax until I know Ian is okay." Julie reached for a crumb-topped apple muffin and peeled off the paper.

"Maybe the FBI can make some arrests with whatever is on the flash drive," Marla said. "Then Ian can come out of hiding."

Julie crossed her fingers. "Let's hope."

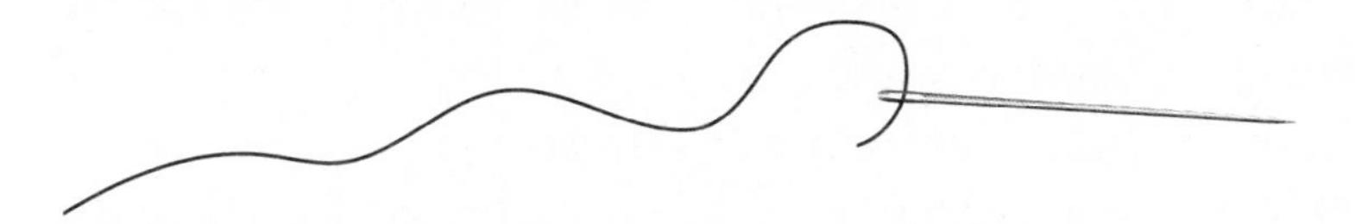

Sofia squeezed another glob of ultramarine-blue paint onto her palette. "What a gorgeous day."

The trio had set up their easels near the water, in a spot with a perfect view of a sailing regatta. Out on the lake, numerous white sails glided along, the crews navigating their watercraft around an island and back toward the marina.

"It really is." Julie turned her face to the sun. "I was so glad to get rid of that flash drive."

The FBI had arrived so quickly that Sofia believed they must have been working nearby. Taciturn as ever, Agent Rico hadn't said much, but Sofia thought she recognized a gleam of excitement in his eyes.

They painted for a couple of hours, lost in the peace and beauty of the setting and the relaxation of painting. Sofia was starting to think about preparing dinner when Marla broke the silence.

"I think our crew is back." Marla pointed to a pontoon boat moving slowly along the shore.

As the boat drew closer, Sofia recognized Matthew and Luke sitting in the bow seat. Mark guided the boat to the dock, nudging it into its berth. Jim jumped off and secured the boat with its bow rope. Tim did the same in the stern. Fergus jumped out of the opposite side of the boat and swam to shore before stopping to shake, spraying the groaning boys in the process.

"Time to fire up the grill, ladies," Mark called.

"I take it you had a good day," Julie called back.

Mark pointed at Luke and Tim. "They did. The rest of us didn't catch a thing."

Luke ran up to Sofia. "Mom, my fish is huge." He put his hands about two feet apart.

"Wow. That is big." Sofia was surprised.

"There are some huge fish out there," Julie said. "Mark caught an eight-pound salmon once."

"I only caught a tiny fish." Matthew's mouth turned down in disappointment. "Dad made me throw it back."

"That's so it can have more time to grow." Jim set down the cooler he was lugging and gave Sofia a kiss. "How was your day?"

Sofia exchanged glances with Marla and Julie. "We'll tell you in a few." She gestured at the boys hovering beside them.

Jim's brows rose. "It must have been exciting. Mark and I are going to clean the fish, then we'll join you ladies on the porch for cold drinks. How does that sound?"

The adults gathered on the porch while the kids played in the water under their watchful gaze.

"So fill us in." Jim stirred his iced tea with a long spoon. "I'm dying to hear what happened."

At Julie's nod, Sofia took Mark and Jim through their visit to the antique shop, the arrival of the thugs, and the visit from the FBI.

Mark heaved a huge sigh. "I hope that's the last of the trouble. If the evidence is on that drive, then the FBI should be able to make some arrests."

"And Ian can come out of hiding," Jim said. "If only we could reach him to give him an update."

"I'll give it a try." Julie picked up her phone. A moment later, she set it down in disgust. "No answer. Yet, anyway."

"All we can do is go about our business," Mark said. "So let's talk about our camping trip to Cow Island. I already checked the weather, and it's going to be perfect."

Marla laughed. "It's really named Cow Island?"

"Funny name, isn't it," Mark said. "An early settler used to take a herd of cows out there in the summer to graze. Unlike most of the islands, it wasn't totally forested."

"The cows were also safe from predators," Julie said. "Now it's owned by the state, and there are a few primitive camping sites you can rent."

"How primitive?" Sofia asked, picturing camping with seven children at a campground with no amenities.

"You should see your face right now," Julie said. "Don't worry, there are bathrooms and water service. Just no electricity."

Mark swirled his glass, the cubes rattling, before taking a drink. "It's one of the few places left to really get away. We don't let the twins bring their cell phones or e-book readers. We try to make it an electronics-free zone. Of course, the adults take cell phones in case of emergency. But we leave them off most of the time."

"That sounds great," Jim said. "Being connected 24-7 is tiring."

Sofia sighed. "I know what you mean." Between the family, her catering business, and community activities, it seemed there were always e-mails to answer and calls to return.

"The kids like it too," Julie said, "after they get over fussing about not having their devices."

"I booked our group for the day after tomorrow," Mark said. "We're taking all three camping areas, so it will be just us out there." He turned to Jim. "You brought a tent and sleeping bags, right?"

"We did," Jim said. "Two tents actually. A large family tent and a small two-person. Sometimes Sofia and I take the small one, and other times we let the boys or girls have it."

"I brought a tent and sleeping bags," Marla said. "And a camp stove. I figured that having one would make cooking meals easier."

"And here I was, ready to cook over a campfire." Sofia pictured herself stirring a huge cast-iron kettle over a roaring fire.

"We toast marshmallows for s'mores," Julie said. "It's a tradition. But the rest of our meals we either eat cold or use gas."

Mark drained his glass. "I think I'll go pull out the camping supplies. I like to air out the sleeping bags for a day or so. They get kind of musty over the winter."

"Good idea." Jim pushed back from the table. "I'll do the same."

"You can hang them over the clothesline out back," Julie said. "Marla's bags are in the storage room too, Mark."

After the men left the porch, the trio lingered over fresh glasses of tea and oatmeal cookies, discussing dinner plans.

"I'll make the grilled zucchini tonight," Sofia said. "That should be good with the salmon."

"And I'll slice some of those gorgeous tomatoes we bought," Marla said.

"That should just about take care of it," Julie said. "If Mark does the fish and we rope the kids into doing the dishes, then I guess I'm off the hook tonight."

"Hey, you deserve a break," Sofia said. "You must be exhausted from worrying about Ian."

Julie pushed her curly hair off her face with a grimace. "I have to admit it, I am. He better never pull something like this again."

Mark appeared in the doorway, a puzzled frown on his face. "Julie, we didn't take any of the gear home with us last summer, did we?"

Julie shook her head. "No. It should all be there."

"I counted everything twice. A sleeping bag and small tent are missing."

"Where could they—" Light dawned on Julie's face. "Ian must have taken them."

Sofia's heart gave a leap. Finally, they had a clue about Ian's whereabouts. "That probably means he's camping to hide out."

"You're right." Julie jumped up from the table. "I'm going to check the canned goods. I bet he took some supplies too. Otherwise, he'd be eating ferns and fish." She paused to stare out at the water glittering in the late afternoon sunlight. "He's out there somewhere. I just know it."

Early the next morning, the loud buzz of a motorboat startled Sofia awake. The engine grew louder, like it was heading straight toward their cottage. Just when she thought it would slam into the shore, it veered off and stopped.

She nudged her husband. "Jim, I think someone is out there."

"Huh? What?" He blinked sleepy eyes.

"I heard a boat stop in front of the cottage."

Jim groaned but pushed himself to a sitting position. "It's probably just a fisherman, but I'll go look."

A fisherman who doesn't mind scaring every fish in the vicinity. Sofia rolled out of bed and followed Jim to the balcony.

Just offshore, a bright-white bowrider rocked in its own wake. A man in sunglasses stood behind the wheel, waving up at them. He was tall and lean with a crew cut, and after a moment, Sofia recognized Thor Anderson, Jim's good friend. Thor was a former special forces operative who owned a security company.

"Son of a gun. He came." Jim moved to the balcony rail and waved back, grinning.

"What's Thor doing here?"

"I called him last night and told him about Ian to see if he could help us find him. He's a tracking expert."

Sofia threw her arms around Jim's neck and squeezed him tight. "What a brilliant idea! Thank you."

A wolf whistle came from the lake, and Jim pulled back, a sheepish look on his face. "I thought you'd be happy. But I didn't want to say anything until I heard from him. Instead of calling, he just showed up."

Footsteps thundered inside, and Matthew and Luke appeared on the balcony. "What's going on, Mom?" Matthew asked. Then both boys spotted the boat and recognized Thor. They flew to the railing, eyes wide.

"Nice boat. Can we go for a ride?" Luke threw his parents a pleading look.

"We'll ask Thor," Jim said. Cupping his hands to his mouth, he called, "Good to see you! After you tie off, come on over. Coffee's on."

Thor raised a hand in acknowledgment and started the engine, keeping it at a low growl. "Where's he going?" Matthew asked.

"I told him he could dock in front of the Butler cottage," Jim said. "Go get dressed, boys, and wash up for breakfast."

"I'm making blueberry pancakes," Sofia said. "Tell your sisters."

"Blueberry pancakes. Wow!" Matthew scurried off, followed by Luke.

To the boys' delight, Thor put away a towering stack of pancakes that rivaled their own consumption. Sofia kept busy cooking batch after batch on the long griddle while Jim poured orange juice and refilled coffee mugs and milk glasses.

"Thanks for breakfast, Sofia," Thor said, his voice a pleasant rumble. "Buttermilk blueberry pancakes with real Vermont maple syrup is one of my favorites."

"Mine too." Matthew's eyes were wide as they fastened on his idol. "Can we go out on your boat today?"

"Matthew," Jim scolded. "Wait for an invitation."

Thor laughed. "It's no problem, Jim. Of course you can go for a ride." He nodded around the table. "So can the rest of you. I was thinking we could break out the water skis later. That is, if you like waterskiing."

A chorus of yeses and whoops answered him.

"I love waterskiing," Vanessa said. "It's almost as fun as snow skiing. And a lot warmer."

Wynter grinned. "I like jumping the wake back and forth."

Vanessa gave her an elbow. "Show-off."

Wynter ducked away, giggling.

Thor set his utensils neatly across his empty plate. "So it's a plan. We'll go out this afternoon."

"Awesome." Vanessa stood and picked up her plate. "Come on, guys. Help me clear the table. Then let's play a game of badminton."

"Boys against girls?" Matthew picked up his juice glass and plate, his fork precariously balanced on the dish, and tottered toward the sink.

"If you want to lose." Luke zoomed up behind him with his own dishes, reaching around his brother to deposit his load.

"We'll toss a coin." Wynter went around the table and gathered the rest of the plates while Vanessa took care of the remaining glasses.

After a few clattering moments and the sound of running footsteps to the front door and down the porch steps, there was blessed silence.

"More coffee, Thor?" Sofia held up the carafe.

"Sure. Thanks." He held his mug out for Sofia to refill. "After we finish up here, I'd like to review my lake charts with your friends."

"We'll go over in a minute," Jim said. "Let me call first to be sure they're up."

"I'll call," Sofia said. Marla and Thor sometimes dated, and she knew her friend would appreciate a heads-up.

"If your friend's brother is out there somewhere, we'll find him," Thor said as Sofia got up from the table.

"I hope we do," Jim said. "There are some really nasty people who are pulling out all the stops to find him first."

14

Titanic
April 13, 1912

After she discovered that the gun was missing, all chance of sleep was lost. Aria moved from seat to seat in the parlor, thoughts and fears jostling in her mind. Had Daisy shot Edward? She appeared genuinely shocked and grieving, but what did that mean, really? If she had done the deed in a fit of passion, she would still regret it. And she was certainly good enough as an actress to pull off a show of innocence.

Guilt writhed in Aria's belly at this disloyalty. How could she doubt her best friend, the girl she had cherished since childhood? Daisy was a gentle soul: headstrong, yes, but not prone to violence. She thrust the suspicions away, hoping she could forgive herself for entertaining them for even a moment.

Then a terrible realization struck her, causing her to stop dead in the middle of the room. Other people had seen the gun. Molly, Patrick, Lady Olive, and Lord Henry. What if they told the captain about it? The fact that the gun was missing wouldn't exonerate Daisy since anyone of sense would have tossed it into the bottomless sea.

Daisy needed help. Someone who would be on her side and not rush to judgment.

Mr. Pierce. He would help them.

She ran to the bell, not caring if it was the middle of the night. This couldn't wait until morning.

A steward she didn't recognize answered her summons, groggy and not very happy about her call. "Can I help you, miss?" he asked as he swayed back and forth.

"I need you to fetch Mr. Pierce." He stared at her, uncomprehending. "You know, the assistant purser."

He blinked. "Oh yes, miss. Is it something that can keep until morning? I'm sure he's abed by now."

"I'm afraid it can't wait. And I don't think he's sleeping, though if he is, wake him. You'll probably find him at the infirmary or with the captain."

His mouth dropped open, but she didn't elaborate, instead practically pushing him back out the door. "Hurry, please. It's a matter of some urgency." Worried that he might gossip, she reached into her pocket and pulled out a pound note. "Keep this under your hat. It's a very delicate matter."

His gaze became knowing. "Yes, miss. I understand." Suddenly jaunty, he tucked the money away and strode off with a smile.

Wonderful. Now he assumed she was seeking a romantic assignation with the assistant purser. Though that was surely more socially acceptable than discussing a murder with him.

She collapsed on the sofa, tension fleeing at her certainty that help was on the way. Somehow, despite their short acquaintance, she knew that Mr. Pierce was trustworthy, a man of integrity, a friend. She leaned her head back and closed her eyes.

A soft knock on the door woke her. Glancing at the mantel clock, she saw she had drifted off for about half an hour.

As she had hoped, Mr. Pierce had arrived. "Miss Greco." His eyes were concerned. "I'm sorry I took so long to get here. I was still tied up with the . . . situation."

"I understand. I'm just grateful you were able to come."

Once he was inside, Aria found herself unable to speak, fear and dismay sitting like a cloying lump in her chest. The whole thing was just too dreadful.

His eyes met hers for a long, fraught moment. "Have you learned something disturbing, Miss Greco?" he asked, his tone gentle.

"Yes, yes I have." Tears burned behind her eyes. "Daisy had a revolver, you see, in her luggage. And it's gone."

He grasped the implications immediately. "Ah. You think that gun was used to kill Edward."

How nice that he didn't leap to accusations against Daisy. "What else can I think? It was there earlier, and now it has disappeared, and a man is dead."

His brow furrowed. "Did anyone else know she had it? Besides you and Miss Griffin, that is." Again, he was careful not to lead her.

"I don't want to point fingers, you understand." She waited until he nodded to continue. "I can't speak to anything that might have happened before the voyage, but I do know who saw the gun today. We used it for an audition, you see."

"An audition? You mean for one of Miss Griffin's films?"

"Yes. Mr. Astor's valet, Patrick, wants to work in films. So Daisy had him act out a scene from a Western scenario I'm writing."

Mr. Pierce sank down onto the sofa without invitation. "Did you say Mr. Astor's valet?" He shook his head. "Oh my."

Aria sat beside him. "I did. And in addition to Patrick, Mrs. Astor's maid was here. Also Lady and Lord Norwich." Had the gun still been out when . . . She couldn't remember. "Mr. Lafitte, the French director, might have seen it as well. Oh, and our stewardess, Molly." She gave a little laugh. "It was like Grand Central Station in here this afternoon, wasn't it?"

Mr. Pierce stroked his mustache, thinking. "This is a tricky situation. I need to proceed cautiously."

Aria guessed his concern. "Why upset prominent passengers without cause?"

"Exactly. Mr. Ismay is right. While justice needs to be served, this situation could easily blow up into a public relations disaster. The company might even be sued if someone is falsely accused. Not to mention the panic on board should news of a murder become common knowledge."

Aria's main interest was in clearing Daisy, but she could sympathize with Mr. Pierce's dilemma. "We'll have to be extremely discreet."

He threw her a puzzled glance. "We?"

"Yes, Mr. Pierce, we. You cannot talk to people without acting in an official capacity. However, I know these people personally and can perhaps discover vital clues through our interaction."

"That is a good point." He frowned. "I don't want to put you in danger, however."

She shrugged. "Don't worry about me. As a writer, I'm practically invisible. Most people don't realize how much I gather through observation and listening. They're just happy to have an audience."

"Hmm. I must confess that being a purser is similar. Many people don't treat me or other staff as if we have ears and brains."

"Yet the servants know everything, don't they? Perhaps their gossip can provide insight as to who killed Edward and why."

"Let's start there, with the staff. Someone had to get in here to steal the gun. Either the key was stolen or one of the stewards let the person in."

"Good point. Shall we call Molly?"

Mr. Pierce glanced at the clock. "It's the middle of the night. Rousing her now will only set off alarms. How about I come back at breakfast?"

Impatience knotted Aria's nerves, but she decided not to press the issue. "I hate to wait, but I suppose you're right." She rose to her feet. "See you around eight? That's when Molly brings us coffee."

Aria didn't sleep a wink that night, but at least she was able to rest her aching body in bed for a few hours. At a few minutes before eight, she rose and dressed, then arranged her hair into a semblance of order. On the way to the parlor, she stopped to check on Daisy.

"How are you today?" she asked her friend, who was huddled under the silk coverlet.

"Terrible. I'm not getting up." Daisy opened one eye. "Please don't make me."

Aria moved to the side of the bed and stroked Daisy's soft, tangled hair. "You don't have to. Mr. Pierce is helping me figure out what happened last night." She paused. Should she tell Daisy about the missing gun? After a moment, she decided she had to. Maybe Daisy had seen or heard something that would reveal who had taken it.

"What is it, Aria? Your face looks strange."

"Stranger than usual?" Aria gave a little laugh. "Actually, Daisy, I have something to tell you. Your gun is missing."

Daisy scrambled to a sitting position. "What? My gun is gone? Are you sure?"

"I checked through the luggage several times. The bag of bullets is also missing."

Daisy flung back the covers. "Someone used my gun to kill Edward." She jumped out of bed. "This is horrible. Who could have done such a thing? They must have been trying to pin it on me."

"Or they took advantage of an opportunity. The gun is gone, probably thrown overboard."

"That's right. I didn't see a gun in Edward's stateroom. Not that I was looking for one . . . but I would have noticed it."

"Mr. Pierce made a thorough search." Aria bit her lip. "I took him into my confidence. He's going to help me find out who killed Edward." A soft knock sounded on the outer door. "There's Molly now. Are you coming out, or should I bring your coffee in here?"

Daisy's shoulders drooped, and she turned toward her bed. "Please bring it in, if you don't mind. I'm really not up to seeing anyone today." As Aria hurried to the door, she said, "But please keep me informed. I have to know who took the life of the man I love."

Molly seemed her usual cheerful self as she served the coffee and toast, laying out the ship's daily newspaper for Aria. She didn't seem to flinch when Mr. Pierce arrived.

"Good day, Mr. Pierce. How are you?"

The circles under Mr. Pierce's eyes revealed his lack of sleep, but he was as well-groomed and dapper as ever in his uniform. "I'm fine. And you, Molly?"

"Very well, thank you, sir." Molly picked up a cup of coffee. "I'll just take this in to Miss Griffin, shall I?" She hurried into the other room, and Aria heard her soft, reassuring tones as she served the hot drink to Daisy.

Aria's belly knotted at the confrontation to come. She liked Molly enormously, and she hated to think that she was somehow involved in this terrible situation. But they had to start with the one person who most often visited their rooms.

"Molly," Mr. Pierce said when the stewardess came back into the room. "Please have a seat." He gestured to one of the chairs at the table.

A look of fear darted across Molly's pretty features. "Is it my work, sir? Am I not up to snuff?" She settled herself into the chair, arranging her skirts and apron.

"It's nothing to do with that," Mr. Pierce said. "We need to ask you something about last night."

Molly studied her apron, pleating the spotless white linen into folds with her fingers. "What do you mean, sir?"

With a glance at Mr. Pierce, Aria spoke. "We need to know if you let someone into this stateroom last night."

The maid's eyes were full of fear. "No, miss. Of course not. I would never do that." She hesitated, her chin trembling. "Is there a reason you're asking me that?"

"Something is missing." At her gasp, Mr. Pierce added, "We don't believe you took it, Molly. That's why we wondered if someone else was in here while the ladies were at dinner."

"Where are the keys kept?" Aria asked. "On your person?" Mr. Pierce probably knew the answer to this, but she wanted to hear it directly from Molly.

Molly shook her head. "Oh no, miss. They hang on a rack at the head steward's station so whoever needs to use them can get to them. Of course, we only use them when we're cleaning or the like, when the guests aren't in their rooms to let us in."

Mr. Pierce examined the young woman for a long moment. "That is all for now, Molly. You're dismissed."

The stewardess jumped up and hurried toward the door, stopping only to say, "Please ring if you need anything else, Miss Greco." Then she fled.

"She knows something," Aria said after the door was safely shut behind her.

"I think so too. But what are we going to do?"

"I'll try again later. Perhaps she'll be more open with just me." Aria smiled at his surprise. "Woman to woman." She added cream to her coffee and took a sip. She needed the beverage's reviving ability this morning for certain.

"I'll leave you to your breakfast," Mr. Pierce said. He turned to go.

"Just a minute, Mr. Pierce. Do you remember the argument that we overheard between Edward and Lord Henry?"

He rubbed his mustache. "I do. Do you think their disagreement escalated to murder?"

"Well, Lord Henry did say he wished he could call Edward to

a duel. At the time, I assumed he had just let his temper get the best of him." Was Lord Henry angry about Edward's involvement with Daisy, perhaps? To all appearances, Lord Henry still loved the actress. Perhaps the prospect of her marrying the millionaire sent him over the edge. Although that would be an extreme reaction for the mild-mannered Lord Henry.

"I think we would have to know more about why they argued." Mr. Pierce smiled ruefully. "Your suggestion of helping me is a good one. I wouldn't know how to broach such a topic with an English peer."

"He's a man like any other," Aria said. "With a man's weaknesses and vulnerabilities. I'll think about how we should approach Lord Henry and the others. Then let's meet later this morning."

His eyes met hers for such a long moment that she felt warmth begin to swarm up her neck and into her cheeks. "I do wish we were meeting for some other purpose."

"So do I, Mr. Pierce," she dared to say before tearing her eyes away. "So do I."

Coffee and toast weren't enough, not this morning, so Aria decided to go to the first-class dining room for breakfast. The maître d' escorted her to a table with two other women. She recognized Lady Duff-Gordon and Mrs. Margaret Brown. He pulled out her chair for her and left with a promise to send over coffee immediately. She exchanged greetings with the other women and then picked up the menu.

Aria scanned the items quickly, marveling at their variety. Everything from oatmeal to smoked haddock to grilled lamb to kidneys. All very exotic, but she just wanted poached eggs on toast with sausage.

"Is it true?" Mrs. Brown asked after the waitress brought Aria coffee and took her order. "Is Edward Thurston really dead?"

Stalling, Aria took a sip of coffee. Here it was already. The trick was not to lie but to omit. "I'm afraid so."

Lady Duff-Gordon moaned as she fanned her face with a menu. "Oh my. His mother must be devastated."

"How is Miss Griffin?" Mrs. Brown's face was sympathetic. "I understand he was courting her."

"She's taking it hard, of course." Aria decided to keep her answers short so she wouldn't inadvertently say too much.

Mrs. Brown leaned forward, lowering her voice. "Did you know he had a heart condition? I never would have guessed. Such a fine figure of a man." She pursed her lips and shook her head, frowning.

"Such ailments hide behind a healthy facade," Lady Duff-Gordon said. She patted her chest. "A weak heart often has no symptoms until the fatal event strikes."

Aria was grateful for Lady Duff-Gordon's explanation. She would use it herself when she was questioned by others. The waitress set a plate with perfectly poached eggs on toast and sizzling, savory sausages. Mouth watering, she picked up her fork and knife and dug in.

She was thankful when the others turned to lighter topics, speaking of upcoming events on the ship and their opinions of the food in the à la carte restaurant. Aria was able to listen with one ear while she ate her breakfast.

As soon as she scooped up the last bite of egg and sausage, she excused herself and left. Several other people tried to catch her eye as she hurried out of the dining room, but she deliberately avoided looking at them. Some of them she hadn't met formally, but her connection to Daisy apparently was common knowledge, and the shock of Edward's death had broken through the usual social barriers.

Noting that church was about to start, Aria joined the procession of worshippers. The hour spent in an atmosphere of faith lightened her heart and boosted her spirits. When services ended, she decided to go back to her stateroom to dress for a trip up on deck for some air.

Daisy's bedroom was still shut, so Aria assumed she was still in bed, the curtains closed. Hiding in slumber, not that Aria blamed her. Perhaps Daisy's feelings for Edward had grown deeper than she knew. Aria's resistance to their marriage appeared even more selfish.

Aria pinned on a hat with a veil that covered most of her face, hoping it would prevent people from recognizing her. She knew they were passing through Arctic waters and that it would be cold, so she put on her thickest coat, the one with the sheared lamb collar.

She was right about the cold, which had deterred many of the regular walkers. Even most of the deck chairs were empty, and in those that were occupied, people were bundled in rugs. Above, the sky was a like a brilliant blue bowl, its very clarity speaking of the icy, clear air gusting out of the north.

Aria tucked her chin into her collar and set off at a good pace, hoping the vigorous exercise would warm her. Breathing deeply, she focused on moving her legs back and forth, emptying her mind of thoughts and speculations. It was a technique she employed when her writing stalled, and she found that after a while, creative thoughts would begin to trickle in. Perhaps insights about Edward's death would come the same way.

Lord Henry was the only person who had displayed overt animosity toward Edward. Although she had witnessed surprised, disdainful looks and disapproval directed Edward's way, his extreme wealth and slickly charming demeanor had deflected most criticism. The murder was a shocking outburst of passion, excessive and seemingly sudden.

But such an act must have origins somewhere, deep within a person who harbored resentment and hatred. Something had triggered a determination to end Edward's life. Was it a recent and atrocious act or a long-simmering grudge seizing an opportunity?

Up ahead, a lone male figure stood by the rail. When he turned his head, Aria recognized Pierre Lafitte. On an impulse, she decided to join him.

"Good morning, Monsieur Lafitte."

"Ah, Mademoiselle Greco. How are you this fine day?" The director smiled, but Aria noticed dark circles under his eyes. Apparently, she wasn't the only one on board lacking sleep.

"I've been better." She moved closer to the rail, gazing down at the glittering wake thrown up by the passage of the enormous ship. Their speed hadn't slowed. The ship was moving toward New York like a horse scenting its barn.

Pierre didn't leap to Edward's death, so perhaps he hadn't heard. He stood in silence beside her, both of them lost in the hypnotic view of rippling ocean stretching to a distant horizon.

"How dark the water is here," he said. "So different from the turquoise blues of the Mediterranean."

Aria sighed, missing the sandy beaches and warm water of the French Riviera. "The North Atlantic is formidable and rather frightening. You couldn't survive long out here."

"Unless you are a whale, perhaps." They shared a laugh at his jest. But then Pierre turned solemn. "Mademoiselle, I am afraid I have done something regrettable."

15

Corinna, Vermont
Present Day

After finishing their coffee, Sofia, Jim, and Thor walked over to Julie's cottage, Thor carrying a roll of charts.

After greeting everyone—including a blushing Marla, cute in pink shorts and T-shirt—Thor rolled out a large nautical chart on the big porch table. "Some people swear by GPS and computerized charts," Thor said, "but I find paper maps more effective for orientation." He slid a hand across the paper's slick surface. "Of course, they need a protective coating."

"So do electronics," Jim said. "Getting one of those wet can be catastrophic."

"True." Thor turned to Mark. "Let's review where Ian might have gone."

Mark moved to stand beside him, pointing out the location of the cottage. "We assumed he went north, toward Canada, but he could have gone across to New York state or farther south in Vermont."

"Yes, he could have gone ashore, or he could be hiding on one of these islands within easy paddling distance." Thor touched several with his fingertip. "The fact that he took a tent and sleeping bag means he planned to camp out. There aren't many places on the mainland to do that without discovery."

"So what should we do now?" Julie asked.

"I say we take my boat around to these islands and check out each one. We'll bring a few of the kids so it doesn't look like a search party. It should only take us a few hours, if that."

Thor's logical assessment made Sofia feel better about the situation, and by the slight smiles breaking out on her friends' faces, she guessed they felt the same.

"We could take the pontoon boat," Mark said. "That's low-key."

"We could, but my boat is faster, and I think we want to quickly rule out the close islands before going farther afield." Thor ran his finger down the length of the lake. "Lake Champlain is huge. It could take weeks to search."

"I don't think we have weeks," Julie said. "Those guys might find him first, or he might starve to death."

Thor snapped his fingers. "Good point. Let's pack some food, water, a medical kit, and blankets. His supplies must be getting low by now."

Julie, Sofia, and Marla put together a picnic lunch along with the items Thor requested. They decided that the boys and the fishing poles would accompany the men on the search party. Fishermen often anchored in the lee of islands, and that would provide perfect cover for a covert reconnaissance.

Vanessa came out on the porch after Thor's boat roared out into the bay. Wynter and the twins trailed behind her. "What can we do, Mom? We're kind of bored with sunbathing."

"We're sick of shopping too, believe it or not." Wynter made a funny face.

Sofia regarded her daughters with amusement. "Why don't you go kayaking? There are a couple of tandem boats, so the twins can go with you."

Vanessa glanced at her sister. "Are you up for that?"

Wynter made a muscle with her arm. "Absolutely. We'll get buff."

"Can I go with you, Wynter?" Ellie asked. "Cindy and I won't be able to keep up with you guys."

"Of course. And Cindy can team up with Vanessa."

The twins clapped their hands and bounced up and down, excited about another outing with the big girls.

"Make sure you stay along the shore," Julie said. "Motorboats can't always see kayaks."

"And wear your life jackets at all times," Sofia said.

"Yes, Mom." Vanessa rolled her eyes. "You always tell us that."

"Hey, I have an idea," Wynter said. "Why don't we paddle up to Corinna's town dock and have lunch? There's a café."

"I'll give you some money for lunch," Sofia said, reaching for her wallet. "Call me when you get there, okay?"

"Thanks, Mom." Vanessa pocketed the bills. "We'll call you, I promise." To the other girls she said, "Let's put our swimsuits on under our clothes."

"They should be safe along the shore, right?" Sofia asked after the girls thundered away. "I hate to be a worrywart, but I hope they don't run into those thugs."

"Understandable, but I doubt those hooligans will be out kayaking," Julie said. "That requires too much effort."

"True." Sofia's phone chimed. "Oh, it's Clara's granddaughter." With all the action around Ian, Sofia hadn't had a chance to schedule a visit with the *Titanic* survivor's descendant.

"Sofia? This is Amy. I haven't forgotten about you. I mentioned your visit to my grandmother, and she's eager to talk to you."

"That's great. I'm glad to hear it." Sofia gave her friends a thumbs-up.

"I wanted to let you know, though, that we're leaving today and will be away for a few days. We're going to a family reunion in Massachusetts. But we can get together when we get back."

"That'll be fine. We're going camping for a couple of days anyway."

Amy mentioned a day and time, and Sofia made a note. "We'll plan on that," Sofia said, "and if you have to reschedule, let me know." She crossed her fingers that they wouldn't have to. Yes, she could drive over from Cabot Falls if need be, but it would be nice to meet Clara while they were nearby.

"Same here. Take care." Amy signed off.

"I hate to say it, but I almost forgot about researching Aria Greco," Marla said. "I guess it's all the excitement."

"You mean the excitement of seeing Thor?" Julie's green eyes danced.

"No, of course not." But Marla's blush gave her away.

"What should we do this morning?" Sofia asked, feeling a little let down as the girls paddled away from the dock. Once again, everyone was off doing something, and they were alone at the cottage.

"I have an idea," Julie said. "I'll run up to the farm and get some fresh cream and fruit. We'll make homemade ice cream."

"If we add eggs, we can make gelato," Sofia said. Her grandmother had taught her how to make it when she was younger, and it had been far too long since she'd made any.

"Oh, that sounds great," Marla said. "We can make different flavors."

Julie rose to her feet, dusting off the seat of her shorts. "It's a plan. Why should the kids have all the fun?"

After Julie returned from the farm with pints of fresh-picked raspberries, fresh eggs, and quarts of cream, they set to work.

"The basic difference is that you make a custard first." Sofia gently stirred the cream and sugar that was heating on the stove. Marla was beating egg yolks in a metal bowl, and Julie was making a raspberry puree in the blender.

"So we let everything chill before putting it in the ice-cream maker?" Marla asked. She pulled the beaters from the eggs.

"That's right." Sofia moved the bubbling mixture from the heat to cool. "After I blend the cream and eggs."

"I'm done with the puree. Now what should I do?" Julie asked.

"Let's start the chocolate custard. We can let that chill in the fridge and make it after the raspberry batch is done."

"Let me dig the cocoa powder out of the pantry." Julie disappeared into the pantry.

"Hello? Anyone home?"

Sofia glanced toward the back door to see a man standing there, pressing his face to the screen.

"Who's that?" Marla asked, fear flashing across her face.

Sofia recognized Jason from the farm stand. "It's okay," she told Marla, moving toward the door to unlatch the hook. "Hi, Jason. Did Julie forget something?" She couldn't think of any other reason why the young man would be there.

"Forget something?" Jason's face creased in puzzlement. "What are you talking about?"

"Julie went . . . Never mind. Come on in." Sofia stepped back to let the young man enter, the screen door squeaking shut behind him.

Julie popped out of the pantry, clutching a brown tin. "I found it. Good thing, because I really didn't want to drive back up to town."

"You're Ian's sister, aren't you?" Jason asked.

"That's right. And you work at the farm stand." Julie frowned. "You're Ian's roommate, aren't you?"

"That's right." Jason glanced around. "Is he here? I saw his car."

Julie set the cocoa on the counter. "Ian is missing. And has been for a couple of days."

"Missing? Oh no. Don't tell me that." Jason collapsed onto a kitchen chair, clasping his hands between his knees. His face was stark white.

"What is it?" Sofia rushed to his side. "Has something happened?"

He looked up at her. "Yeah, you could say that. Some goons just trashed my apartment. They were looking for Ian." Relief flashed in his eyes. "That means he's probably okay, right?"

"We hope so," Julie said. "We think he could be camping on one of the islands." Joining Jason at the table, she quickly took him through the sequence of events. Sofia meanwhile blended the cream-and-egg mixture and set it to cool on top of a bed of ice before joining the others.

"So what happened with the goons?" Sofia asked. "Did they drive a sedan?"

"I don't know. I didn't see the car. Two guys knocked on my door early this morning, and I stupidly answered. They busted right in and started tossing the place, asking me about Ian."

"What did they look like?" Marla asked.

By the description Jason gave, Sofia believed they were the same men who had come down to the cottage. "You really should call the police, Jason."

"No, he should call the FBI." Julie rose. "Let me get Agent Rico's card."

Jason's hair practically stood on end. "The FBI? What the heck is Ian involved in?"

"We're not sure," Marla said, "but it's something to do with his job."

"Did they take anything from the apartment, Jason?" Sofia asked.

"They took Ian's laptop. Fortunately, mine was in my car. Otherwise, I'd be sunk. I'm taking classes, and all my homework is on it."

Julie returned, carrying the business card. "Please call them. They'll be eager to talk to you."

Jason took the card and studied it. "I suppose I should." He pulled out his phone and entered the contact info. "I'm going to go over to the farm and stay there until this mess is settled."

"Good idea," Sofia said. "I hope those men won't bother you again."

Jason stood, tucking his phone in his shorts pocket. "I hope not too." His glance fell on a green pint of raspberries. "You get those from us? Good choice." On the way out the door, he stopped. "Hey, I just thought of something. You said he might be on one of the islands. Ian was always bugging me to go camping with him on Cow Island. Do you think he's there?"

"I doubt it," Julie said. "You have to make reservations to stay there. We made ours months ago."

Jason shrugged. "Oh well, it was a thought. Call me when he shows up, okay?"

After he left, they went back to making gelato. Sofia mixed a chocolate custard and, after cooking it, set it in the fridge to cool. By then, it was time to churn the raspberry vanilla. Sofia took the custard off the ice and poured it into the ice-cream maker.

"Do you have those raspberries to add?" Sofia asked Julie.

"I will in a second." Julie picked up the pint, dumped the raspberries into a colander, and began rinsing them in the sink. She gasped, one hand flying to her mouth.

"What is it? A bug?" Marla asked.

"No bugs. But I just realized something. Ian can't be staying on Cow Island. It's too busy and monitored by a ranger. But there is a small island nearby. I bet he's there. On Calf Island."

Titanic
April 13, 1912

Aria's heart raced at Pierre's words. Was he confessing to killing Edward? She glanced around. No one was in the area, although she did spot a crew member some distance away, near a row of lifeboats. Would he hear her if she called?

"What do you mean, monsieur?" Aria asked. Noticing a squeak in her voice, she winced.

"I am speaking of my treatment of Miss Griffin."

"Oh." Aria expelled a breath she hadn't realized she was holding. "What do you mean?" Again her voice squeaked, and she deliberately took in several large breaths of air, attempting to loosen her tight chest. Although relieved she wasn't about to hear an admission of murder, she was also disappointed. *That would have been too easy.*

"I seem to be constantly apologizing, don't I?" He chuckled. "But my mama taught me to take responsibility for my misdeeds. And I find I sleep much better when I do." He ran one glove along the brass rail as though testing its smoothness.

Not eager to listen to the inner workings of his conscience, Aria considered excusing herself. Only courtesy compelled her to stay, but refusing to prod him, she kept her eyes on the water and waited.

He sighed deeply. "I must say this. I regret trying to bully

Mademoiselle Griffin into honoring her contract. It was wrong of me to attempt to force my will on such an artistic and sensitive person."

Was he sincere, or was this merely another ploy to manipulate Daisy? Aria studied his profile, the melancholy set of his expression. "I am glad to hear you say that. Perhaps you can have Pan-Francais stop sending unpleasant letters to her."

He waved a hand. "Of course. I will tell them to release her entirely from her obligation. What good would it do to compel her to act in my films? You cannot coerce genius to perform; it must flower freely."

"I will tell her that. Thank you." Aria would hold him to his word.

"When you do, also tell her that I still care for her."

His voice was so low that it took a moment for the words to sink in. "I had no idea that you and she . . ."

"No one knew. It was all too brief." His chuckle was a rumble. "I wanted more, of course, but she . . . she regretted it immediately."

Pierre rubbed a hand over his face, his shoulders bowed, and Aria guessed how much such a confession cost him. Now she understood why Daisy was determined not to have anything to do with the director or his company.

Aria touched his sleeve. "I'm sorry. I will convey your sentiments with discretion."

"Merci, Mademoiselle Greco. And regardless of what transpires between your friend and me, I would still like you to write for me. We are expanding west, to Hollywood, next year."

"Thank you, monsieur. I appreciate that." Aria turned to go but stopped. Now that they were on a better footing, she hated to do this, but she had to. She turned back. "Did you hear about Edward Thurston?"

"What about him?" Pierre continued to gaze at the ocean.

"He is dead."

That bald statement caused him to whip his head around. "What? What happened?"

She studied his face carefully, measuring the shock in his eyes, the puzzlement in the slackness of his chin. He wasn't lying. "It's tragic. His . . . heart just stopped." *Caused by a bullet striking his chest.* "Daisy is inconsolable. They were very good friends."

"*Mon dieu. C'est terrible.* When did this happen?"

"Last night, late. The doctor isn't sure of the time."

"Now I know why . . ."

"Why what?"

Pierre shook his head. "Why he didn't come to breakfast." He put a fist to his mouth as if nauseated.

"When did you last see him?" Aria was almost convinced that Pierre had nothing to do with Edward's death, but she needed to be certain.

"Last night. Right after I left your cabin, I went to see him. He had indicated he might invest in some films. I wanted to discuss that possibility in more depth today." He stepped away from the railing, hands clenched, ready to do something, anything. "His poor mama. I must go extend my condolences. *Excusez-moi, s'il vous plaîs.*" With a tip of his hat, he strode away.

Aria watched his figure recede into the distance, satisfied that one acquaintance had been cleared. Despite his affection for Daisy, Pierre hadn't killed his rival. She would bet on it.

Back at the cabin, all was still and quiet. Aria crept into Daisy's room. The actress was still curled into a ball. Was she going to stay there all day? In a sudden decision, Aria pulled open the curtains, allowing dazzling sunlight to enter the dark room. With satisfaction, she saw a shaft of light touch Daisy's face.

Daisy groaned and threw an arm over her eyes. "What are you doing? Go away."

Aria stood over her friend, hands on hips. "I'm not going away until you get up and have breakfast. I'm not going to allow you to sink into one of your despondent moods. Remember what you told me?" Last time that had happened, Daisy had been melancholy and listless for weeks, and after the spell was over, she had made Aria promise to never let her succumb again.

"I was wrong. And I wasn't grieving then."

Aria reached down and stroked Daisy's hair in the same way she might comfort a child. "I know. But I don't think Edward would want you to wallow. He'd want you to find out who did this horrible thing and bring them to justice."

Daisy opened one eye, peering up at Aria from the shelter of her forearm. "You're right. But I must wear black, all black. Although I wasn't his official fiancée, I loved Edward."

Aria helped Daisy sit up. "Of course. Perhaps you can receive visitors here, in deference to your loss."

A cheeky grin crossed Daisy's face. "I'd offer to sit with Edith, but last time I saw her, she was ready to throw me in the brig for murder. I think I'll avoid her for a bit."

"The story is that Edward died of a heart attack, and be sure to stick to it. We don't want to give away the real cause of death, at least not until the captain and Mr. Ismay are ready to reveal it."

Daisy's brow furrowed in a frown. "Of course I can manage that. I'm an actress, remember?"

Aria sighed. "How could I forget? I'll ring Molly. She can bring you breakfast and help you dress. I must go find Mr. Pierce."

"Thank you for seeing us, Mr. Lafitte." Mr. Pierce and Aria were visiting the French director in his stateroom.

"It's not a problem, I assure you." Pierre gestured at the sofa and chairs in the small sitting area. "Please, sit."

Aria perched on an armchair, as did Mr. Pierce, leaving Pierre the sofa. After they all sat, there was silence for a long moment. Finally, Pierre asked, "What is it that you wanted to talk to me about?"

"I'm sorry, Mr. Lafitte," Mr. Pierce said. "I'm trying to figure out how to approach a difficult topic."

"And what is that, pray tell? There isn't a problem with my bill, I assume, since you brought the lovely Mademoiselle Greco with you." Pierre's mustache lifted as he threw Aria a smile.

Mr. Pierce sighed. "No, my inquiry concerns Edward Thurston's death." At Pierre's exclamation, he held up a hand. "Yes, he died of a heart attack, but there are . . . there are things missing from his cabin. Valuable things, according to his mother." He nodded as though confirming the story with himself as well as Pierre.

Pierre spread his hands wide. "What does that have to do with me?"

"Nothing, of course" was the quick reply. "But Miss Greco told me that you visited Mr. Thurston last night, and we hoped that perhaps you saw someone else either leaving or going to the cabin."

Pierre rubbed his chin. "I see your point. You think someone might have taken advantage of the man's death to rob him? *Exécrable!*"

"You're right," Aria said. "It would be. Er, was." At her blunder, she ducked her head and prayed Pierre hadn't noticed.

"As I told Miss Greco," Pierre said, "I went to see Edward last night to set a breakfast appointment. Lord Norwich was there, having a drink with him."

Aria and Mr. Pierce exchanged glances. Lord Henry had argued with Edward previously. Had their disagreement escalated?

"Did you see anyone else around? In the corridor, perhaps?"

"Lurking, you mean?" Pierre shook his head. "*Non*. I saw Lady Norwich go to her cabin. And there were servants going back and forth." He shrugged. "In and out of rooms, as expected."

"You don't remember which ones particularly?" Aria asked. Even if Lord Henry was the guilty party, they could question others in the vicinity about what they may have seen or heard.

"I'm afraid not. I wasn't really paying attention." He waved a hand. "They were, as you say, part of the background. The scenery."

Mr. Pierce's chin lifted. "I understand perfectly."

Outside Pierre's stateroom, Aria stopped Mr. Pierce. "What shall we do next?"

Seeing a pair of passengers coming along the corridor, Mr. Pierce took her arm and steered her into an alcove. "I must tell Captain Smith and Mr. Ismay about Lord Norwich's visit with Mr. Thurston." He threw a hand in the air. "I am sure Mr. Ismay will be beside himself. Questioning an English lord, no less."

"I have an idea," Aria said. "I'll invite Lady Olive to lunch in our cabin. Maybe she can provide some insight into what happened last night."

"She won't want to implicate her husband."

"No, but if she's like most people, she's dying to unburden herself. And learn what she can from us." Aria recalled the avid interest from Mrs. Brown and Lady Duff-Gordon at breakfast. Surely Edward's death was the talk of the ship, at least in first class.

Taking her arm again, Mr. Pierce guided her down the hallway. "Let me know what happens." He sighed. "I do have to report our conversation with Mr. Lafitte to the captain. He may want to interview Lord Norwich."

"I'd love to be a fly on the wall for that." She cocked her head and smiled. "You don't suppose they'll let me sit in?"

Mr. Pierce patted the hand tucked through his arm. "I'll try, Miss Greco. But I'm sure they regard a murder inquiry as inappropriate for a lady."

"What do you think, Mr. Pierce?" Aria found herself batting her eyelashes, a very uncharacteristic gesture.

He leaned his head closer. "I think there is no one I would rather have assisting me."

"In that case, please call me Aria."

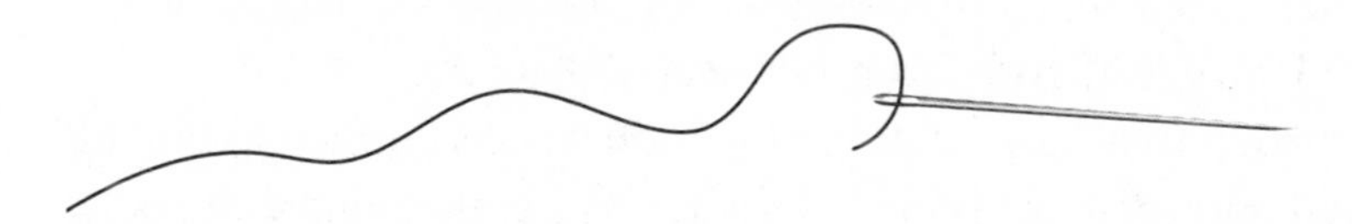

Warmed by her new friendship with Mr. Pierce—Charles, as she now knew him—Aria found herself strangely cheerful during lunch. Aria did her best to hide her buoyant mood in front of Olive and Daisy, both sunk in gloom. With reluctant appetites in mind, Aria had chosen lobster bisque, green salad, and fillet of sole for lunch, a light but tasty and nutritious meal. A stewardess named Bertha brought the food to the stateroom.

"Where is Molly?" Aria asked the stewardess.

"I am afraid she is ill," Bertha said. She placed the food in front of the three ladies. "Please ring for me if you need further assistance, miss."

Aria tried a bite of the salad. "Do try this dressing." Aria pushed the sauceboat toward Olive. "It's very good."

Olive picked up the dish and drizzled dressing on her salad. "Nothing really tastes right to me, I'm afraid." The pretty brunette had lavender circles under her eyes, and her movements were slow and languid.

"You knew Edward quite well, didn't you?" Daisy asked. "Didn't he attend your wedding?"

Olive gave a hollow laugh. "I guess you could say I knew Edward very well indeed. We once were engaged."

Daisy dropped her soupspoon, sending droplets of bisque onto the tablecloth. "What? You were engaged?" Her blue eyes snapped with outrage. "Why didn't I know about this?"

Olive's lip curled, and her eyes flashed. "You didn't care to avail yourself of my castoffs?"

Aria tensed, poised to step in. She moved the bread basket aside, since Daisy had been known to toss rolls in frustration.

Daisy half rose from her seat. "Of course not! I am just surprised that Edward didn't mention it. I certainly told him all about my romantic history." Daisy's cheeks pinked, and she pressed her lips together. Aria wondered if she included her dalliance with Pierre in that recitation. She thought not.

Olive picked up her fork and stabbed at her salad. "Edward had a habit of keeping secrets. Most of them wore skirts." She jabbed a tomato and held it up as if it were an exhibit. "Don't feel bad. You're not the only woman he lied to."

Daisy sagged back into her chair, a hand to her brow. Aria recognized the pose from one of her films. "Now you're telling me he was a liar and a scoundrel? Was our whole romance an illusion?"

Olive's tone was deadpan, which made her words all the more cruel. "Probably. I'm not surprised he died the way he did."

A chill ran down Aria's spine. The cause of Edward's death was a secret, shared only by a few. Did Olive know who shot Edward? Or—

"What do you mean, the way he died?" With an effort, Aria kept excitement out of her voice. She longed to reach across the table and shake the truth out of the other woman. She must know something.

Dismay flitted over Olive's face, followed by a placid smile. "He had a heart attack, right? How fitting for the man who broke mine."

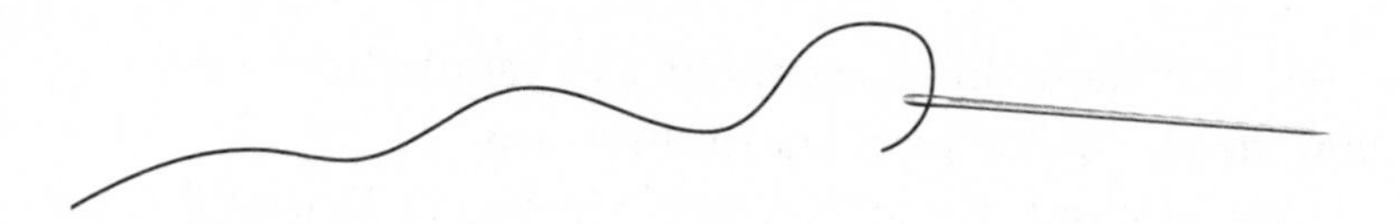

The rest of the day and most of the next were a blur for Aria. Between Charles's purser duties and Aria attending to the needs of Daisy and Mrs. Thurston, they barely saw each other. So Aria arranged to meet him the next evening after dinner. Daisy refused to leave the stateroom, so Aria decided to accept Lady Olive's invitation for the à la carte restaurant. After debating what to wear, she finally chose the new Lucile dress, feeling as though she were going into battle and that elegant garment was her armor.

"I'm with Lord and Lady Norwich's party," she told the maître d' stationed at the entrance.

He bowed. "Very good, madam. Follow me."

As Aria wove through the tables, she noticed the captain was the guest of honor for a large, lively group. Mr. Ismay and the doctor were seated at a table for two.

"Just a minute," Aria said. She stopped by Mr. Ismay's table. Both men stood.

"Good evening, Miss Greco," Ismay said. "So glad you could join us this evening." The doctor echoed the sentiment.

After Aria returned their greetings, she asked, "Is there any progress in the matter of poor Mr. Thurston?"

Ismay blanched, his eyes darting left and right as though worried about being overheard.

Dr. O'Loughlin stepped in. "Everything is as it should be. A most unfortunate event, one that our first-class passengers don't need to be concerned about. We will handle things once we reach New York."

Aria heard the subtext: *In other words, butt out.* They weren't going to risk the reputation of the ship by disturbing their elite clientele with something so grubby as a murder investigation, even if the victim had been one of their own.

"I understand. Good evening, Mr. Ismay, Doctor." Aria nodded and swept away, anger coiling in her belly. *How dare they sweep such an event under the rug?* Then a stab of guilt panged. By not reporting the missing gun to the captain, she was equally duplicitous in trying to spare Daisy suspicion and scandal. The only possible solution was to discover the killer before they docked in New York.

Consumed with her thoughts, Aria barely paid attention to the lush repast. Caviar, lobster, quail. They all passed in front of her like a dream. Her dinner companions were equally quiet. Only the bright conversation of Mrs. Brown indicated that anyone at their table was still alive. Finally, dessert was served, and after a bite of an éclair, Aria thanked her hosts and made her escape.

As arranged, Charles was waiting at the foot of the Grand Staircase as the clock at the top chimed eleven times, crying out the lateness of the hour. Aria was gratified by the way his eyes lit up when he spotted her. "You look lovely tonight, Aria," he said, taking her hand in his.

Warmth flooded Aria's face at his compliment. "Thank you, Charles. It's one of Lady Duff-Gordon's creations."

"I wasn't speaking of the dress, although it, too, is quite stunning." He stared into her eyes for a long and meaningful moment. "Why don't you get your coat and we'll walk on deck?"

After stopping by the stateroom, they went outside, Aria's arm tucked in his. When the frigid air hit her face, Aria shivered, grateful for the soft fur around her chin. "It's even colder than earlier today."

"Hovering right around freezing. We're in iceberg territory." He pointed to the mast. "It's the job of the man in the crow's nest to keep a lookout."

Aria gazed out at the black ocean. The night was sparkling clear, stars freckling the heavens above. "It's a lovely night, even if it is cold." How much of her comfort had to do with the man next to her? Something new and exciting sparked between them, unspoken but as real as the frost-tinged breeze.

For a few minutes, they stood side by side at the rail, absorbing the evening's beauty. Then Charles spoke. "At my insistence, the captain and Mr. Ismay questioned Lord Norwich today. I said they had to, since he was perhaps the last person to see Mr. Thurston alive."

Aria's pulse raced. "What did he say?"

Charles grunted. "Not much. He claimed they were discussing a private matter that had no bearing on Thurston's death."

"And they accepted that? Why, Lord Henry threatened to challenge him to a duel!" Aria was outraged. "I learned something interesting today at lunch with Lady Olive. She was once engaged to Edward."

"Do you think their argument involved her?"

"I don't know. Lord Henry also courted Daisy, so that is another connection between the two men." Should she share Olive's unpleasant insinuations? They were rather indelicate to discuss with a man. She cast through her mind for a way to frame the issue. "Lady Olive also implied that Edward was not a man of honor. How did she put it? He had secrets, and most of them wore skirts. She was quite bitter."

"Ah. That could have bearing on the case. Perhaps Mr. Thurston was still making advances to his former fiancée."

"While courting Daisy? If that is so, I would kill him myself."

"You are a feisty lass." Charles patted her hand. "They regard murder as a man's crime, but perhaps it was a wronged woman after all."

"Olive seemed to know, or at least suspect, that Edward didn't die of a heart attack." Aria imagined the woman stealing the gun and hiding it among her skirts, then going to Edward's stateroom to confront him regarding old wrongs. She shook herself. "But why would she kill him? She is married now."

"It is a puzzle. We can only hope new information will come to light before we reach New York." He turned his head. "On another, more pleasant topic, I wanted to ask . . ."

"Yes?" Aria nestled closer to his warm bulk.

He took such a deep breath that Aria felt his chest expand. "May I court you in New York?"

Joy bubbled inside Aria's chest. "Of course you may. But I may not be staying in New York."

He pulled back slightly. "What do you mean? Are you going back to Boston?"

Aria shook her head. "No, I will probably be headed to Hollywood. It's the new center for movies. Mr. Lafitte wants to hire me to write scenarios for his company. And I think Daisy will be going there too, now that Edward is gone."

"Hollywood? Perhaps I shall try my luck there as well."

Aria laughed. "There aren't any ocean liners there. It's all desert and farmland."

"I'm going to leave the White Star Line. It's time to try something new."

Aria's heart sang. "Really, Charles? I would love that."

"Really." He tugged her away from the rail, turning to face her. He stepped closer, gathering her in his arms. "May I—"

Overhead, a bell rang three times.

Aria was startled. "What's that?"

Charles pointed. "Iceberg. Straight ahead."

They stared in shock and disbelief as the white obstacle loomed ever larger in their path. The great ship began to turn, the engines groaning at the strain.

"It looks like we're going to miss it." Relief filled the purser's voice as he hugged Aria tight. "Thank God."

Then they felt a bump and heard an eerie scraping sound.

Charles remained stoic, but in her heart, Aria knew the truth. The *Titanic* was in trouble.

17

Corinna, Vermont
Present Day

"All set, everyone?" Mark called out. "Here we go!" He started the pontoon boat engine and slowly backed away from the dock. Sofia braced herself against the railing, where she stood next to Jim and Marla. The camping gear and food was heaped in the center of the boat, presided over by Julie. The rest of the crew was lounging on seats around the outside of the large boat, Fergus shadowing Matthew and Luke as usual.

"Yay! We're going camping!" Matthew gave an exuberant leap from his seat, bumping into Luke, who slipped sideways, catching himself with a hand on the rail.

"Be careful, Matthew," Jim warned. "No horsing around on the boat."

Sofia was grateful Matthew was wearing a life jacket. Once she was certain he had settled down, she turned her attention to the wide expanse of lake, silvery under an early morning sky. In the east, a smudge of tender pink faded as the hot yellow ball of sun nudged above the mountains.

"A great day to be out on the water," Jim said. He lowered his voice. "I sure hope Julie's theory is right."

The expedition with Thor to the other islands had been fruitless. Calf Island hadn't been on their original list. Once they were set up on the larger island, they planned to paddle over to Calf Island to look for Ian.

Sunlight glinted off something across the lake, flashing into Sofia's eyes. *What was that?* It shone again, and she elbowed Jim and pointed.

He put a hand to his forehead and squinted. "It's sun bouncing off something. It must be another boat."

Probably just another fisherman, that's all. Sofia leaned against the railing, forcing herself to enjoy the fresh, fragrant day and the excitement of their outing. But worry festered, souring her stomach. *Those men looking for Ian haven't given up,* she sensed. The menace of their presence troubled her like a far-off rumble of thunder. It felt as if something ominous were rolling around in the distance.

Julie opened one of the baskets and pulled out a thermos. "Coffee, anyone?" She set it on the deck and dug out a stack of paper cups.

"I'll take some," Sofia said. They'd gotten up at five so they could get under way by six. Far too early for her taste.

"Is there anything to eat?" Matthew asked, joined in a chorus by Luke and the twins.

Marla laughed. "Are you sure we brought enough food, Julie?"

"We have tons," Julie said. "I take normal consumption and triple it. Camping seems to make everyone hungry." She pointed to a sack. "There are muffins in there. Vanessa, you're closest. Please pass some around."

Sofia sipped her coffee, enjoying the warm cup against her chilled fingers. She hoped they had brought enough warm clothes. Yes, it was summer, but nights and mornings could be cold as the season slid toward fall. Just a couple more weeks and it would be time for back-to-school shopping.

She halted the progression of her thoughts. *Enough of that.* She needed to enjoy the here and now.

As the day warmed, other boats appeared on the lake, buzzing in all directions. The pontoon boat was ponderous and slow, but it was stable and comfortable, like a floating patio. For the most part, the kids were relaxed, content to watch the water passing.

"How much farther?" That was Matthew. He had held out for almost an hour.

"See that island right there?" Mark pointed. "That's Cow Island. We'll be there soon."

Matthew scrambled to the seat in the bow, dangling his legs through the railing. "I can't wait. I'm going to put up my tent and then go fishing."

"Sounds like a plan, bud," Jim said. "I'm looking forward to some more fishing myself."

As they passed another island, a motorboat came racing around from the other side, going so fast it was slapping up and down on its own wake.

"He's going too fast," Mark said. "Don't ever do that, kids."

Instead of veering away as expected, the boat continued to come straight at them.

"What the heck is he doing?" Jim waved his arms. "Slow down."

"Doesn't he see us?" Julie asked.

Mark blew the boat horn, a deafening blast that certainly alerted most of the lake to their presence. The other boat slowed, but it continued to head their way.

As they drew closer, Sofia recognized the occupants—the threatening men who had come to the cottage and the antique store. There was no avoiding them since the much slower boat could never outrun a speedboat.

"Those guys are jerks!" Matthew shouted. "They're bothering us." Beside him, Fergus sat up and barked.

"Hush, boy," Luke said, patting the dog.

"They are jerks." Jim put his hands on his hips and glared as the other boat turned to cut them off. Their wake rolled toward the pontoon boat, making it bob and lurch.

"Hang on, everyone." With a muffled exclamation, Mark cut the engine.

"Ahoy there!" one man called, waving his arm.

Sofia dug in her shorts pocket for her cell phone. "I'm calling the Marine Patrol."

"Good idea," Julie said, pulling out her own phone. "I think I have their number in here."

"Hang on, ladies. I don't think we'll need them."

"What do you mean?" Sofia asked.

"Look." Jim beamed with satisfaction. "He said he'd be watching us, and his word is as good as gold."

Another boat came racing from the shelter of an island, moving so smoothly it appeared to skim across the water. Even the three thugs appeared impressed.

"That's Thor," Luke said, dancing in place. "Yahoo!" He pumped one fist, joined by the other kids, who jumped up and down and screamed.

The men in the other boat caught on that something special was happening and watched in trepidation as Thor's boat roared up, stopping so perfectly that his wake was only a gentle wash.

"And that's how you do it," Mark said.

"Is there a problem, gentlemen?" Thor called, his white teeth gleaming. Sunglasses covered his eyes, and he wore a T-shirt and shorts. Another man dressed the same way stood beside him. Their caps read *Special Ops*.

The men in the other boat looked at one another, shrugging. "No, I guess not," the driver said.

"Then I think you'd better let these folks get on their way." Thor pretended they were interested in his hat. He took it off and studied it. "Like it? My commanding officer gave it to me the day I got my last medal." He settled it back on his head with a grin.

After a long stare-down, the driver started the motor and backed the boat far enough away that Mark could move the pontoon boat. Sofia held her breath as they headed away from the other two boats. When she glanced back, she saw that Thor and his friend were still sitting there, not budging. The other men finally gave up and headed in the opposite direction, north toward Burlington.

"I hope that's the last we've seen of them," Sofia whispered to Jim.

He put an arm around her shoulder and squeezed. "I doubt it. But at least Thor is on the job."

Julie overheard. "And looking pretty good in that Special Ops hat." She whistled, giving Marla a cheeky grin.

Marla pretended great interest in the water flowing past the boat, but Sofia noticed her cheeks were red. "Hamburgers tonight you think, Sofia?" she asked.

"Sounds good. We can roast the corn in the husk in the campfire." Controlled campfires in special pits were allowed on the island. Many campgrounds had banned them.

They traversed the remaining distance to Cow Island without incident, pulling up at the wooden dock to unload. A female ranger came down the planks to greet them. "Butler party?"

"That's us," Julie called cheerily. Opening the pontoon boat gate, she clambered out onto the dock to sign the paperwork and accept the list of rules. Sofia climbed out, noticing that the island was still mostly field, with copses of evergreens and other trees here and there. Several small brown buildings stood a short distance away. The washhouses and community cabin, Sofia guessed.

The ranger glanced at Fergus, who had disembarked and was sniffing at her shoes. "Good thing your folks have the place to themselves, or we wouldn't be able to keep you around," she said, bending down to pat the dog.

"Fergus is a really good dog," Matthew said. "He scares bad guys."

"That's a very good trait for a dog to have," the ranger said. "Do you and Fergus want the grand tour?"

"You bet. Come on, Fergus." Matthew slapped his thigh, his signal for the dog to walk beside him. Once everyone got out of the boat, the ranger led the way to the campsites, showing them the amenities along the way. The washhouses had composting toilets, low-flow showers, and an area to wash dishes. Barrels filled with gathered rainwater from earlier storms was the only source, so they were urged to conserve water. The community cabin had a huge fireplace and was stocked with sporting goods, games, a table tennis set, and books.

The campsites were set throughout a small forest that provided shade and cozy nooks for their tents. In the middle was the stone-lined fire pit, already supplied with a stack of wood.

"Douse your coals at night," the ranger said. "We don't want any forest fires."

"There's not much of a forest on this island," Matthew said.

"No, there isn't," the ranger agreed. "But it would take many, many years for big trees to grow again."

"Yeah." His freckled face was thoughtful. "And the buildings might burn too."

The last spot on the tour was a lighthouse, placed on a spit of rocks to warn sailors about some dangerous shoals off the island. The squat white tower consisted of spiral stairs leading up to a small room ringed by a deck. There was just enough room for their group to gaze out at the view.

"There's Calf Island," Julie said, pointing to a small round island between Cow Island and the New York shore.

From their vantage point, it looked entirely wooded except for one rocky outcropping. Sofia couldn't see any sign of a person or a campsite. Was Ian there? If so, he was well hidden.

"I'm leaving the key with you," the ranger said to Mark and Julie. "You can come back up here later, but please leave it clean."

"We will," Julie promised.

After one last admonishment to pack out all their trash, she wished them well and headed down to the dock, where she got into her motorboat and roared away.

After exiting the lighthouse, the kids ran around the sites, arguing over who was going to pitch their tent where.

"No one is sleeping anywhere until the tents are set up," Jim said. "So let's go, troops. Bring everything up here."

By the time they had set up the camp, Thor had arrived with his companion, Jed Bates.

"Want some lunch, Thor?" Julie asked, looking up from the sandwich assembly line on a picnic table. "Turkey with Swiss or ham with American?"

"Yes," Thor said, making the boys hoot with joy. Anticipating her next question, he added, "With mustard and mayo."

"You got it," Julie said.

Thor winked at Marla, who went scarlet. "Chasing bad guys is hungry work."

"That's what Fergus says," Matthew said. "Mom, can Fergus have a sandwich?"

"No, Matthew. He is only supposed to eat his kibble and canned food."

Luke elbowed his brother. "You know that already, silly."

The kids picked their lunches first, taking their sandwiches, chips, and drinks down to the dock. The adults sat around the picnic table to talk while they ate.

"I think a small team of us should go over to Calf Island," Thor said. "That's it over there, right?" He pointed to a land mass to the left.

"Yes," Julie said. "You know, there's a cave on that island. Maybe Ian is staying there."

"That's right," Mark said. "That would be a perfect place to hide."

"I'll stay here with the children tonight," Jed said.

"Me too." Jim's lips were set in a grim line. "Just in case those clowns show up again."

"Oh, they will." Thor's eyes glittered. "But we'll be ready for them."

"Let's hole up in the lighthouse," Jed said. "That's certainly easily guarded."

"Good idea," Thor said. "I'll call in a couple of other men too."

After lunch, Julie, Mark, Sofia, and Marla went down to the dock to get into Thor's boat. The children almost mutinied, but Thor promised them a ride once they got back.

Calf Island was only minutes away, but there wasn't a dock. Thor dropped anchor as close as he dared, then they had to wade to shore. Sofia was glad she had on her water sandals since the bottom was rocky and slimy.

"Which way to the cave, Julie?" Thor asked once they were all onshore. "Do you remember?"

Sofia hoped so, since a thick wall of trees and undergrowth confronted them.

"It's basically like bushwhacking through the jungle," Julie said. "We found it by accident one day." Hands on hips, she stared around before striking off into the brush. "I think it's this way."

The rest of the group followed Julie, making slow progress while stepping over logs, skirting bramble patches, and ducking under branches. Within fifteen minutes, Sofia was hot and sweaty, with scratches on her legs and arms.

"Maybe we should have stayed with the kids," she said to Marla.

Marla pushed back her tangled hair. "It would have been easier. But not as exciting."

A shout came from up ahead. "That sounds like Julie."

They hurried through the remaining woods as fast as they could, heedless of the rocks and limbs in their way. With a final burst of effort, they emerged into a small clearing carpeted by green ferns. Straight ahead was a huge boulder, and standing in the cleft of the rock was Ian. Or at least she guessed it was Ian, from the little she could see thanks to Mark and Julie, who had him in a joint bear hug.

"I am so glad to see you all." Ian's smile was bright against the stubble on his chin. "You say that the FBI has the evidence? That's awesome."

"You can come back home now," Julie said.

Thor put up a hand. "Not so fast. Ian is still in danger until those thugs have been arrested. Even if the FBI has the evidence, there may be reprisals against him."

Julie looked sick. "Really? That's horrible."

"Thor is right, Julie," Ian said. "My old boss is a snake. I've seen his vindictive side in action."

"What do you suggest, Thor?" Mark asked.

Thor moved to each corner of the small clearing, thinking. Then he pulled a piece of paper out of his pack, using it to draw a map of the island. "All right, folks. I have a plan. But first, Ian, does your cell phone have any juice?"

Ian's shoulders slumped. "No. I tried to conserve as much as I could, but it's an old one, and it dies fast."

"If that's the truth, then maybe I can forgive you for not calling me." Julie cuffed her brother lightly on the shoulder.

"I'd have liked to call you, honest, but I was also afraid they might track me through the GPS."

"Let me see your phone," Thor said. He studied the configuration of the ports and then pulled a square red box out of his pack.

"What's that?" Mark asked.

"A hand-crank radio and charger," Thor said. He rummaged through his pack pockets and pulled out a charger that he used to connect the phone. He cranked away for a couple of minutes. "That should be enough." He powered on the phone and handed it to Ian. "Call your boss and tell him that you'll give him the evidence if he'll call off the dogs."

Ian took the phone reluctantly. "He'll never do that."

Thor smiled, a sharklike grin. "That's what I'm betting on."

From her perch on a boulder, Sofia could see the crackling flames of a campfire and smell fragrant smoke drifting through the trees. She hoped the men stalking Ian would see it as well.

A mosquito whined near her ear. She swatted at it, thankful she had worn long sleeves and pants. Otherwise, her bare skin would be a feast for the hungry critters. Except for the yellow fire, the darkness in these thick woods was nearly complete. She hoped that meant she was invisible.

In her mind's eye, she pictured the island. She, Julie, and Marla were stationed around the perimeter as lookouts. The men were guarding the main path, which had been widened and set with snares and nets. Thor was convinced they would land in the spot he had chosen earlier, since the shore wasn't as rocky there.

Over on the main island, the kids were up in the lighthouse, and once in a while, she could hear their excited voices calling and shouting. They were thrilled at the idea of sleeping up there and had readily abandoned the tents for the night.

A motorboat engine echoed in the quiet night air, approaching the island at a steady speed. Then it slowed to a troll, humming along for a few minutes. Silence. Splashing and the quiet murmur of voices.

Sofia tensed. The men were here, lured by the phone call and the fire, as Thor hoped. She prayed that the men would be captured quickly, without incident. Holding her breath, she strained her ears, hoping to discern from the rustle and snaps of underbrush where they were.

Fear flooded her body. The intruders were coming right toward her.

18

Titanic
April 15, 1912

Charles hugged Aria tight, holding her until the icy monolith floated by into the night. Chunks of ice littered the deck, shed from the berg as it passed.

"What's going to happen now? Is the ship going to sink?" Aria's voice rose to a shriek as terror flooded her body.

He stroked her hair gently. "No, my dear. This ship is built to be unsinkable. But I must go to the bridge and learn the extent of the damage. Go to your stateroom, and I'll come as soon as I can."

Aria clutched at his sleeve. "Please do. I'm petrified."

Charles kissed her on the cheek, his lips warm against her frozen skin. "Everything will be fine." With his arm around her shoulder, he guided her along the deck to the entrance door. "Will you be all right from here?"

"Yes, of course." With a wave, Aria darted into the passageway, all senses on alert. The impact didn't seem to have been noticed by anyone inside. Elegantly dressed men and women still promenaded up and down the Grand Staircase. Strains of orchestra music drifted into the corridor from the lounge. Deep within the ship, the motors still thrummed, although they had slowed.

The hallway leading to her stateroom was deserted, since passengers were either in bed or still socializing in the public rooms. She unlocked her door and slipped inside. All was quiet, with only one lamp burning in the parlor. Not bothering to switch on another light, she put down her key and hurried into Daisy's room.

Leaning over her friend, she shook her shoulder. "Daisy, Daisy. Wake up. It's an emergency." Despite Charles's reassuring words, Aria was reluctant to believe that the ship was still seaworthy. They needed to be awake and alert just in case.

She had to shake Daisy several times before she opened her eyes with a groan. "What is it, Aria? I finally got back to sleep just a few minutes ago."

In the light streaming into the room from the parlor, Aria noticed traces of tears on Daisy's cheeks and felt a pang of sympathy. Daisy must have cried herself to sleep while Aria was eating dinner and walking with Charles.

"I'm sorry, Daisy. But the ship hit an iceberg, and you must get up."

"What are you talking about?" Sitting up in bed, Daisy craned her head back and forth. "Am I still asleep and dreaming? I thought you said the ship hit something."

"It did. Charles and I saw it happen. We scraped along the side of an iceberg. Big pieces of ice landed on the deck right next to us."

"But nothing seems to be wrong." She cocked her head. "I don't hear anything. No alarms, no screaming."

It was true. The ship was almost eerily silent. "Maybe it wasn't badly damaged. Charles has gone to find out."

Daisy smiled. "Charles, is it? I take it you're talking about Mr. Pierce."

Aria played with her silk skirt, unable to meet her friend's eyes. "Yes, I am. He wishes to court me."

"That is wonderful. He is a fine man." Daisy gave Aria a huge hug. "I am so happy for you." She pulled back. "Does this mean you are retiring from writing?"

"Never. I can't do that. I love it too much. Charles is planning to leave the ship and go to Hollywood. He wants to do something new."

"That sounds like a wonderful idea. I've heard Hollywood is booming. They'll need all sorts of workers in the film industry, not just actors and writers. Though he could act. He's handsome enough."

Her friend's approval warmed Aria. "I'm so glad you like him."

"Unlike the way you disapproved of Edward."

Aria flinched at her caustic words. "I'm sorry. I know you cared for him greatly."

Daisy sighed. "I thought I did, but now I believe I was building romantic dream castles. I think I was seeking an escape from acting. I've been doing it for so long, and I'm so very tired." She sighed again. "I saw what I wanted to see. Olive's confidences slapped me like cold water in the face. Edward wasn't a nice man, not really."

"Be that as it may, he didn't deserve to be murdered. Charles and I have been trying to find out who did it since the captain and the ship's owner don't seem to be interested. Not if it inconveniences the rest of the passengers."

Daisy laughed. "Really? How brave of you. You're like a Pinkerton detective."

Aria rose to her feet. "I don't know about that. But listen, you'd better get up and dressed. Just in case the ship is in trouble."

As if in response to her words, a thunderous knocking sounded on the stateroom door. Aria ran to answer. Charles stood there, gasping with exertion. In contrast to his neat appearance earlier, his face was red and his uniform coat askew. His hat was missing, and his hair stood on end.

"You must get your life belts and go up to the deck," Charles managed to gasp out. "Five of the airtight compartments were breached, and the ship won't stay afloat for very long."

A strange, hollow calm settled over Aria. The worst had happened. This beautiful, unsinkable ship was on its way to the bottom of the frigid sea. Visions of swirling black waters filled her mind. *Will drowning hurt very much? Or will I freeze first?* She sent up a mute prayer for mercy.

Charles touched her shoulder. "Aria. Did you hear me? You must come quickly." He gave a strangled sob. "There aren't enough lifeboats."

A few minutes later, Aria and Daisy left their stateroom, dressed in their warmest coats and wearing life belts. Next door, a steward was knocking on the stateroom door. When the sleepy occupant answered, the steward said, "Put on your life belt, sir, and go up to the boat deck."

"But why? It's the middle of the night." Dressed in a nightshirt, the man ran a hand through his hair.

"It's merely a precaution, sir. You'll be back in bed in no time."

"That's not what Charles said," Daisy whispered. "Do you think he's wrong about the danger?"

The cold dread in her belly told Aria otherwise. "I think they're trying to prevent a panic."

Daisy called out to the steward. "Is everything going to be all right?"

"I'm sure of it, miss." He moved along to the next door. His wide eyes and greenish complexion said something different.

A crowd was milling around in the first-class lounge, driven inside by the extreme cold out on the deck. Some still wore evening garb while others were dressed in their nightclothes. Only a few wore life belts. In the corner, the orchestra played dance music.

"Aria, Daisy. What's going on?" Olive wandered up to them, wearing a life belt tied over her dressing gown. "I'm thinking about going back to my stateroom." She tugged at the belt. "This seems foolish."

"Don't do that, Olive," Aria said. "The ship hit ice. I saw it. Wait a little longer." She was hesitant to raise the alarm since a panicked crowd was a dangerous one.

"If you say so." Olive turned and pushed her way through the crowd. As she went, Aria noticed that her feet were bare under her nightgown.

"Where's Edith?" Daisy asked. "I don't see her anywhere."

Aria studied the crowd, concurring with Daisy's observation. The elderly woman wasn't in the room, and without her son, she had no one to help her during this emergency. "I'll go to her cabin and see if she's still there."

"I'm coming with you."

Aria was amazed at Daisy's offer. "Really? After the things she said to you?" The elderly woman adamantly believed that Daisy had killed her son.

"What does that matter now? We may not survive the night. Our disagreements seem rather petty in light of that."

Aria had to agree with the truth of that statement. Nothing mattered now except helping their fellow passengers survive.

They fought their way through the thickening crowd to the lounge doorway, a matter of fighting the tide of passengers coming the other way. They hurried down the Grand Staircase to their deck, ignoring those who called out to them to stop, to go back upstairs to safety.

"I have a feeling we're going the wrong way," Daisy said.

"Does the floor seem tilted to you?" Aria wasn't sure if she was imagining things, but when they reached the bottom of the staircase, she felt like she was walking on a slight incline, uphill away from the bow.

"It definitely is." Daisy went to the French doors leading outside. "See? The horizon isn't level." She was right. The line of black ocean against a star-filled sky was definitely slanted.

Aria's supernatural calm fled at this simple evidence of the boat's demise. She pictured the bow of the boat tipping farther and farther down as water flooded the lower decks. Soon it would dive toward the bottom.

Her heart began to beat painfully fast, and she started running. "Hurry, oh please, hurry. We need to make sure we get a place on the lifeboats before they're all gone."

The hallway was deserted, and their footsteps thumped as they ran to the last room, where Edith was staying. Aria banged on the door. "Edith! Edith! Open up." She had to knock on the door a number of times before she finally heard shuffling footsteps approaching.

The door opened a crack, revealing a slice of Edith's cream-covered face and slumber cap. "What is it?"

"Edith, the ship is sinking. You must come with us. Right now."

Edith opened the door wider, frowning when she spotted Daisy. "I'm not going anywhere with that woman." She wore a floor-length nightgown and wool slippers on her feet.

"There's no time for such delicate sensibilities," Daisy said. "You need to come with us. There isn't much time left."

"Are you telling the truth? They told me this ship was unsinkable." Edith abandoned the doorway and began to dither about her stateroom, wringing her hands. "Of course, I never expected to have my son murdered on this floating palace either."

Aria moved into the room, glancing around for Edith's life belt. "Why would we lie? Look at us, we're wearing coats and life belts. The assistant purser is a good friend of mine, and he told me five compartments were breached. There's no hope for the ship." She found the white life jacket on top of the wardrobe. "Come on, put this on so we can go back up on deck."

Edith continued to moan and waffle, so Daisy went to the wardrobe and dug out her coat and warm boots. "You must put these on right now or else we'll hold you down and do it."

The older woman allowed Daisy to slide her arms into the coat sleeves. "What about Edward?" she whispered. "Are we going to leave him behind?"

Aria and Daisy exchanged glances. Edward's body was somewhere in the ship's hold, and it wasn't feasible to try to retrieve it.

"I'm afraid we must," Daisy said, her hand gentle as she straightened Edith's collar. "Sit down and I'll help you with your boots."

Edith plopped into a chair, and Daisy knelt in front of her, boot in hand. "Take your slipper off, that's it. Now point your toe."

Edith obeyed, and soon both boots were on. Daisy reached her hand out to help the older woman up.

"I misjudged you, my girl." Edith's voice was husky. "You didn't have to come back down here at your own risk to rescue an old woman."

"Yes I did," Daisy said. "I loved Edward, and I know you did too." She put her arm around Edith. "Now let's fly."

The elevator wasn't working anymore, so they had to help Edith climb the staircase step by step with the use of her cane. The older woman appeared weaker and more fragile under the stress of the night's events, but her tart tongue wasn't impaired, Aria noticed to her amusement. As a young man pushed past on the stairs, knocking them aside, Edith called, "It's women and children first, you ninny. Unless you consider yourself a child?"

He threw them a wide-eyed, blank stare and fled, obviously out of his mind with fear.

"They don't make men the way they used to, and that's a fact," Edith said.

As they entered the lounge, Aria noticed that almost everyone was out on deck. Even the orchestra had moved and was playing outside. "What's going on?" she asked a steward rushing by.

"They're loading the lifeboats." He raised his voice. "Women and children, women and children, to the lifeboats please."

"I told you." Edith's tone was rich with satisfaction. Tapping her cane, she made her way toward the open French doors.

Charles appeared, his dear, familiar face beautiful to Aria. "There you are. You must go out and get in a lifeboat."

On deck, the dense mass of people surged and swayed, their wide-eyed fear and braying voices reminding Aria of cattle she had once seen herded toward slaughter. A flare shot up and burst overhead, joined quickly by another and another. Distress signals. Was anyone out on the dark ocean to see them?

"Women and children!" a man bellowed. "Are there any more women and children?"

"Go," Charles said, pushing them toward the rail, where crewmembers were loading a lifeboat. He kissed Aria on the mouth. "I love you. Don't ever forget that." Then he vanished in the crowd, leaving her glowing and bereft.

"Charles! Charles, come back!" she shouted. *Will I ever see him again?* she wondered. And then, just as quickly, *No, not in this life.*

"Come on, Aria." Daisy was guiding Edith forward, her body protectively sheltering the older woman. "We have to get in the boat."

Reluctantly, Aria obeyed, forcing herself to join the line waiting to load. Once again she went numb, knowing that if she allowed herself to feel a grief barely held at bay, she would go mad.

Painful dramas were going on all around them. "No, I won't leave you!" a woman cried, clinging to her husband's lapels.

"You must, sweetness. You must." Tears ran down the man's face.

A young dandy in evening dress tried to cut the line, only to be repelled brutally by a crewman. Aria recognized the man from the stairs. The crewman pulled out a pistol and waved it at him. "Get back, you coward. Women and children only."

A baby screamed in her mother's arms, the shrill wails piercing through the crowd's shouts and cries.

Lord Henry appeared at Aria's elbow as they neared the railing. He threw her a frantic glance, calling, "Daisy, Daisy."

Daisy turned her head. "Henry. What is it? Where is Olive?"

He shook his head. "I must tell you the truth. Now, before it's too late."

"What do you mean?" Daisy's blue eyes widened.

Before Henry could answer, the crewman used his body to forcibly block his advance. "Get back, sir. Stand back." Within seconds, Henry was lost in the milling crowd. Daisy and Edith were next in line, and a man in uniform helped Edith climb into the boat.

Another flare went off, illuminating the deck like a fireworks display. In the momentary glare, a movement near a bulkhead caught Aria's eye. Two little girls huddled together, the older one with her arms around the younger. Both wore hair ribbons and white frocks, inadequately dressed for the bitter night. Aria spoke to the woman with the baby. "I'm going to see about those girls." She pointed.

"Please hurry," the woman said, clutching her own child fiercely.

Aria walked over and hunkered down to talk to the girls. "Where are your parents?"

The older one stared at Aria, her lips trembling. "We don't know. We can't find them." Aria guessed she was about six or seven years old.

"Mama," the younger girl sobbed, fisting both eyes. "I want Mama."

Aria held out her hands. "Come with me. We'll find them later."

They stood up and took Aria's hands, their tiny fingers clasping hers in poignant trust. The trio slipped back into line, just in time to board the lifeboat.

Aria peered over the rail, her belly contracting at the sight of the dangling craft swaying on its ropes, the bottomless ocean a dizzying distance below. But the span from the deck to the water was visibly shortening minute by minute as the ship settled in the water.

Holding her breath and praying she wouldn't slip and fall into the water, Aria clambered down into the boat. Then she reached up her arms to catch the girls. They landed safely, and Aria sat on a hard wooden bench, tucking them close beside her. Someone handed her a blanket, and she draped it over her shoulders and wrapped it around them. Across from her, Daisy and Edith huddled together under their own blanket.

"Women and children! Any more women and children?" someone barked on deck.

A few more women joined them, the others shifting on the benches to make room, and then a pair of crewmen boarded to man the vessel. Then came the order to lower the boat.

"Godspeed," someone called. "May the Lord bless you and keep you."

Aria's eyes burned with tears as she looked up at the people lining the railing. Face after face staring down at them. How many of them would survive this night? A knife twisted in her heart at the thought of each soul perishing so horribly.

The ropes jerked, and the lifeboat began to descend. For good or ill, Aria and her companions had left the magnificent, doomed vessel known as the *Titanic*.

19

Titanic,
April 15, 1912

Aria held the girls tightly as the boat made its lurching journey down to the water. They landed with a splash and sway, then the crewmen and some of the women picked up the oars and began to stroke strongly, sending their small craft skimming away from the ocean liner.

Nearby a woman was praying under her breath, and Aria found herself silently joining in. What would become of them now? How long could they survive, exposed in such bitter weather?

"What's going to happen to us?" Daisy asked the nearest crewman.

He paused momentarily. "They've sent a wire to the *Carpathia*. She should be arriving soon."

"Will they get here in time?" Edith asked quietly. "In time to save the others?"

"I don't know, mum." He began to pull the oars again.

Aria couldn't tear her eyes away from the *Titanic*. Despite the pronounced forward list, almost every porthole and public room above the water level shone with light. Masses of people surged about every deck, and the ship's band was playing heartfelt hymns on their stringed instruments.

The next couple of hours were a nightmare almost too great for human hearts to bear. While Aria and the other passengers watched helplessly, the great ship continued to sink into the black water, deck after deck vanishing. The captain called through a bullhorn for the lifeboats to return to pick up more passengers, but theirs was full to capacity.

"Why don't they go back?" Aria cried. "I don't understand."

"They don't want to be swamped, miss," the crewman said. "The big boat is likely to pull them under when she goes."

"There goes our room and my Lucile dress," Daisy said when first class disappeared below the waves. "Do you think we can get a refund?"

Everyone laughed, the levity, poor as it was, relieving their torment for a moment.

A woman screamed. The ship had tipped forward so far that the stern was thrust up into the air. A thunderous roar and screams were heard as the contents of the ship crashed forward. People jumped or were thrown from the boat into the water. Cargo floated in the water everywhere: a piano, deck chairs, boxes, and trunks. The last lights on the *Titanic* blinked and then extinguished. The forward funnel broke off, crashing into the ocean and smashing anything in its path.

The great ship then broke in two with a horrendous groaning and squealing of metal. The bow sank, and the stern floated for a minute before it, too, disappeared beneath the water.

The occupants of the lifeboat screeched in horror, shaking at the abominable sight. Aria clutched the girls harder, tucking their heads under her arms, hoping they were too young to realize what had just happened. She fixed her gaze on the terribly empty spot where once the ship had rested, sorrow for all the lost souls flooding her heart.

She allowed herself a moment of private grief, for Charles and for what might have been.

For a while, cries and shouts came from the water, but gradually those stopped, leaving the lifeboats floating in a dark and empty sea, hoping for rescue.

"We're going to die too!" someone wailed.

"Make your peace with God. That is all we can do," said another.

"Miss Greco. Miss Greco," whispered a voice behind Aria.

She half turned to see their stewardess, Molly, huddled with a blanket over her head. Joy surged in her heart. "Molly! You're alive!"

"I am thus far, thanks be to God." She ducked her head. "But I must tell you something so I can make my peace."

"What is it, Molly?" Aria wondered at the girl's choice of confessor. Surely her sins must be insignificant anyway.

"I let Patrick into the cabin, miss. He took the gun."

At first, Molly's words didn't penetrate. Her concerns about Edward's murder had receded, like something that had happened to someone else. Understanding dawned. "You're saying that Patrick killed Edward?"

Daisy and Edith gasped. "Who is Patrick?" Edith asked.

"He's Mr. Astor's valet," Molly said. "Apparently, his sister was dishonored by Mr. Thurston. Or so he told me."

"That makes sense." Aria thought about Olive's claim that Edward was a philanderer. His misdeeds had finally caught up with him.

"My son was a sinner, no mistake," Edith said. "But he didn't deserve to die that way."

"No, madam, he didn't," Molly said. "And now justice has been served to his killer." She clutched Aria's arm. "Do you think God will forgive me?"

"Of course He will, child," the praying woman said. "Just ask Him."

Everyone fell silent, lost in their own thoughts and prayers as they waited for rescue—or death.

When the lights of the *Carpathia* appeared, Aria thought she was dreaming. She had nodded off a few times, awakening each time with a wrenching pang of loss.

"Is that a ship?" someone asked.

"It is. It really is!"

A palpable sense of excitement grew as the lifeboat's occupants realized their prayers had been answered and rescue was at hand. Aria burst into tears of gratitude. For whatever reason, she had been spared. She prayed silently, vowing, *I will make the most of this undeserved gift.*

Healing sunshine poured down on the *Carpathia*'s deck, warming the clusters of *Titanic* survivors scattered among the other passengers. Leaning back in her deck chair, Aria turned her face to the rays, heedless of the sun's effect on her complexion.

Joy thrust a bright tendril through her dark weight of sorrow. Charles was alive. By some miracle, he had been pulled from the water by another lifeboat. Suffering from hypothermia and frostbite, he was in the infirmary but was expected to recover.

So many other women weren't as fortunate. They had lost husbands, fathers, fiancés, and friends. She turned her head to check on Daisy and Edith, who sat in chairs beside her. Edith was asleep, snoring as would not befit a lady. Daisy read a book under the shelter of a parasol.

"How are you doing?" Aria asked Daisy.

Daisy put a bookmark in the novel and closed it with a sigh. "I'm just reading the same words over and over." She gazed out at the horizon, where gentle waves rippled. They had left Arctic waters behind and were sailing in the warm Gulf Stream. "I keep reliving that terrible night."

"I do too. But then I force myself to think about what remains, the many blessings I'm grateful for."

"Like Charles?" Daisy beamed. "I'm so happy for the two of you."

To Aria's surprise and discomfort, tears welled. They seemed endless lately. "I am so blessed. I don't deserve it."

Daisy reached over and patted her hand. "Stop feeling guilty. You and Charles can spend your lives helping orphans or something."

That was a thought. Aria's eyes fell on the Bannister girls playing nearby. Etta and Edna, as they were called, had relatives waiting for them in New York. Otherwise, they would have been sent to an orphanage. Maybe she and Charles could adopt orphans. Well, at least one. She hoped they would have children of their own.

One positive effect of the sinking had been the rapid escalation of their courtship. They had gone from walking about to engaged within a day.

And some poor women had gone from wives to widows in the same span of time.

Aria's heart clenched in sympathy when she saw Lady Olive wandering toward them. Her hair was down, flowing over her shoulders in a tangled mess. She wore a hodgepodge of donated clothing, including a dress that was much too large.

Olive veered in their direction, her borrowed boots clumping. Rescued barefoot, she had been lucky not to lose a toe or two. Reaching their chairs, she sat down on the deck.

"Olive. How good to see you." Daisy's voice was warm.

In response, Olive hunched her shoulders and stared at the boots. More than one rescued passenger was suffering from a lapse of sanity. Was Olive one of them? Leaving her be, Aria watched the Bannister girls run and shout instead. The enviable resilience of children.

"I'm sorry, Daisy." Olive's voice was a low murmur. "Please forgive me."

"What was that?" Daisy adjusted her parasol against the sun's new position. "You have nothing to be sorry for."

"But I do." Olive took a deep, shuddering breath. "It was me, you see, who sent those notes. And the bouquet of dead flowers."

Scarcely believing her ears, Aria pushed herself to a more upright position. "You did that, Olive? Really?"

Olive's face twisted. "I was jealous. Henry always loved you best, Daisy."

"That can't be true." Daisy's protest was hearty.

"Oh, but it was. I knew that from the beginning. At first, I thought I could handle that, but after a while, it wore on me. And then when we saw you in Monte Carlo . . . I became somewhat deranged on the topic." She tried to smile.

"I'm sorry," Daisy said. "I swear I didn't—"

"It wasn't your fault. I know you didn't lead him on or anything—now. At the time, I was convinced that you were trying to seduce him behind my back."

Daisy twirled her parasol with a laugh. "Oh my."

Aria thought about Henry's approach the night of the sinking. Had he been going to declare himself to Daisy? What a disservice he had done by marrying Olive while in love with another woman. How terribly unfair.

"Now I realize how petty such things are." Olive bit her lip as she gazed out to sea. "If only, if only . . ."

Aria wracked her brain for words of comfort, knowing how inadequate they were. She was certain Olive would love again, and she hoped that this time, the man would be worthy. But how could she say that?

She was thankful when a distraction diverted the conversation. A puzzled look passed over Daisy's face as she stared at a woman walking by, wearing a shawl over her head and voluminous skirts. Daisy leaned forward and squinted, then shook her head.

"What is it?" Aria asked.

"You'll think I'm mad, but that woman looks just like Patrick."

"You mean the valet?" Aria leaned forward in her seat and studied the figure standing at the rail. When she turned her head and Aria glimpsed a rather strong profile, she gave a shout of surprise. "That's because it *is* Patrick." What a rascal, dressing in women's clothing to escape detection. Is that how he had gotten a seat on a lifeboat?

Patrick glanced over his shoulder. Seeing three sets of eyes fixed on him, he sprinted down the deck, skirts flying.

"He can't go far," Daisy said with satisfaction. "That's one advantage of being on a ship."

Indeed, it took only a shout to a pair of crewman and the valet was soon captured, found hiding in an upside-down lifeboat. At Daisy's suggestion, they brought him to the captain's office.

"What's he done, Miss Griffin?" the captain asked.

"I have done nothing." Patrick twisted and squirmed, trying to free himself from the crewmen's restraining arms.

One crewman snorted. "Except dress in women's clothing. That's worth a year in the brig."

"We believe this man murdered Edward Thurston on the *Titanic*," Aria said.

"Really?" The captain's eyebrows rose. "I didn't hear of any murder on board the ship."

"I am an eyewitness," Daisy said. "I saw his body with my own eyes."

"As did I," Aria said. "Along with his mother." She turned to Patrick. "We could bring her in here, but you might not leave alive."

The captain hid a smile. "I can understand the wrath of a mother losing her son. So, Miss Griffin, take me through what happened."

Daisy succinctly relayed the events of that night, her explanation supplemented by Aria, who concluded, "The captain was in the middle of an investigation led by Mr. Pierce—who is in your infirmary—when the ship sank."

"You don't have proof I took the gun." The handsome valet's face distorted in a snarl.

"But I do have a witness. Excuse me." Aria went to the door. "Molly, you can come in now."

Patrick deflated when he saw the young stewardess, and by the time she finished her story, he had confessed to killing Edward. As Molly had said, he was enraged by how Edward had disgraced his sister, who had then committed suicide.

"Your anger at your sister's fate at Mr. Thurston's hands is understandable, Patrick," the captain said. "And perhaps a judge will be lenient. However, wearing a woman's clothes to escape from a sinking ship? That is the height of cowardice." He gestured at the crewmen. "Take him to the brig."

"Thank you, Captain," Daisy said after the men left. "I was afraid justice would never be served for Edward. He was . . . a good friend."

The captain showed them to the door. "Glad to be of service, Miss Griffin. Let me know if I can be of any other service."

"You can do something for me," Aria said. "Isn't there a minister on board? If not, the ship's captain will do. A young man in your infirmary is about to become my husband, frostbite and bandages or not."

20

Corinna, Vermont
Present Day

Sofia prayed she was wrong. Maybe it was only her imagination that the men were headed right toward where she was hiding.

A large branch cracked and a man swore. "Watch out. You almost got me in the face."

"Sorry. But what do you expect, stumbling around in the dark like this?"

"Can't we turn our headlamps on?"

"No, we don't want Ian to see us coming."

"Then quit talking."

Each word of the whispered conversation confirmed her fears. They were getting closer to her with each step. If the trajectory she imagined in her mind was correct, they would pass right by her. What should she do? If they discovered her, they might run away, and the mission would be a failure.

All she had with her was the can of pepper spray Thor had given her. In order to use it, she would need to be pretty close. An idea niggled in the back of her mind. As quietly as possible, she slid off the boulder and into the ferns.

A big stick has to be around here somewhere. She groped in the bushes and found one of the perfect length and thickness. Hunkering down, she waited.

She measured their progress by the lead man's heavy breathing and grunts. When he lumbered by the big rock, she thrust out the stick, right in his path.

"Ugh." His ankle hit the wood, and he lurched forward, flailing his arms. His toe hit a rock, and he fell flat with a grunt. The other men didn't have time to react, and they stumbled over his body and also fell, landing on him in a pig pile of yells and complaints.

Sofia fumbled at her neck for the whistle Thor had given her and blew an earsplitting shriek. Then she leaped from behind the rock and doused the writhing heap with a large dose of irritating spray for good measure.

Flashlights beamed through the woods, and a helicopter whirred overhead, a searchlight streaming down. *That must be the FBI.*

"Good job, Sofia," Thor said. He and several operatives surrounded the men, training weapons on them. "Don't move, boys. The jig is up."

The helicopter crew included Agents Rico and Barnes, who landed in the only bare spot on the island. Once confronted by the feds, the men were eager to implicate Ian's boss, claiming that they only wanted to talk to Ian. But the rope and guns they carried told a different tale.

The Marine Patrol showed up to take the men into custody. Ian went back to Burlington in the helicopter, glad to be released from his self-imposed exile.

Back on Cow Island, their path took Sofia, the Butlers, and Marla by the lighthouse, where the children were sleeping. As they passed by, a sleepy Matthew called out. "Hey, Mom. Can Thor give us a ride in the helicopter?"

They all burst out laughing. "So much for a covert operation," Mark said.

"I'm excited about this," Julie said as she pulled up in front of Clara's farmhouse. "I hope she knows something about Aria Greco."

Sofia hoped so too, but she realized that it was very unlikely that Clara's mother had crossed paths with Aria, or if she had, had thought to mention it. "I would love that, but I'm just grateful to learn more, even if it isn't directly about Aria." She opened the car door and stepped out, excitement bubbling in her veins.

"Don't forget I have that call in to a film historian," Marla said as she slid out of the backseat. "He's promised to give us a list of every film Aria wrote and see how many are still available."

"That's something to look forward to." Sofia took a deep breath and began trudging across the gravel toward the back door. "But I'm so glad this worked out."

Amy answered the door, letting them in with big smiles. "Kettle's on," she said. "And Clara is on the sun porch. She's been talking of nothing but your visit for days."

Sofia laughed. "I'm glad she feels that way. We're excited too."

"It always amazes me," Amy said, leading the way, "how much the *Titanic* continues to fascinate people."

Clara, a slight, elderly woman with a puff of white hair, was seated in a wicker rocker. She held out a hand as they entered. "Thank you for coming to see me."

"I'm so glad you have time for us." Sofia shook her hand and introduced herself, Julie, and Marla. They settled on wicker chairs and a sofa while Amy left to make tea.

"So, I understand one of you had a relative who survived the sinking." Clara's faded blue eyes studied each in turn.

"That would be me," Sofia said. "My grandmother left me a quilt, you see, made up of fabric from throughout our family's history. The quilt was sewn together by my great-great-grandmother, Maria Greco, after the fabric had been gathered for centuries." She turned to Julie and Marla. "I meant to tell you that. At the end of the diary I found a note from Maria, who I gather was also Aria's mother." She turned back to Clara. "Aria Greco sailed on the *Titanic*."

Clara gave a scream. "Amy! Amy! Quick. You have to hear this."

Amy came running. "What is it, Gran? Are you all right?"

"I'm better than all right. This young lady is related to Aria Greco."

"Oh." Amy's mouth opened. "Wow. That's amazing."

Sofia was puzzled. This reaction, while gratifying, didn't really make sense.

"What's going on?" Julie asked.

"You'll see." A sly, sweet smile crossed Clara's face. "Amy, fetch me the journal, will you?"

"I'll do that. First, let me bring in the tea. The kettle's boiling." Indeed, they could hear the whistle all the way from the kitchen.

After settling a tray with teapot, cups, cookies, cream, sugar, and lemon in front of Julie, whom Amy had designated to pour, Amy darted back out of the room. Sofia was left to accept a cup of tea while squirming with curiosity.

Amy carried an old cigar box into the room and set it on Clara's lap. Clara opened the box, releasing a scent of lavender, and pulled out a small journal. "This is the story of my mother's rescue," she said. "Listen carefully and see what you hear." Again she flashed that sweet, sly smile.

Sofia settled back in her chair against the cushions. Glancing at her friends, she saw they wore intent expressions as Clara began to read.

My name is Etta Bannister. When I was six and a half years old, I crossed the Atlantic on the Titanic from England, where we had visited Mother's relatives.

We were all so excited to sail on the Titanic's maiden voyage—Mother, Father, my younger sister, Edna, and me. It was a glorious ship . . .

Etta went on for a bit about the ship's features and how much fun she and her sister had swimming in the pool, playing games on deck, and eating in the dining rooms. Sofia got the sense that the girls hadn't been spoiled exactly, but they had been indulged.

Clara's tone sobered when she reached the fateful early morning hours of April 15, 1912.

Edna and I were in bed when the orders came to go up on deck. My father, God rest his soul, refused to believe there was any danger at first. He left the stateroom, and when he didn't come back, my mother began to panic. Miss Moody, our governess, came in and tried to help Mother get dressed. Then Miss Moody offered to take us up on deck. I didn't like her. She was mean, and my childish doubts were soon justified.

The boat deck was pandemonium. People pushing this way and that, flares going off, lifeboats being loaded. Miss Moody jumped into a lifeboat and told us to wait for our mother. We hid in a corner and waited and waited, but our mother never came.

"That's horrible," Julie said, breaking into the narrative. "She must have been terrified."

"Everyone was," Clara said. "Afterward, on the *Carpathia*, there were many children and even babies reunited with their parents. Etta and Edna weren't among them." She bent her head to the book again.

> *I don't know how long we waited, but suddenly an angel appeared. She had dark hair and was so pretty and kind. Miss Aria Greco, I later learned.*

Sofia gasped, tears in her eyes at hearing her ancestor's name. Clara smiled, putting up a hand. "Just wait."

> *Miss Greco quickly grasped that we were alone, and seeing that the last lifeboats were filling up, she took us with her. It was scary climbing down into the boat, but once we sat down, she put a warm blanket over her shoulders and hugged us to her. I'll never forget the sense of love and safety she provided.*

> *We were among the last people off the ship. Fortunately, both my sister and I were so exhausted that we didn't witness the terrible last moments of the Titanic. I've tried not to think about it too much, about the terror and fear my poor parents faced. All I can hope for is that I'll see them again someday in Heaven, where I believe they wait, smiling down on us, as thankful for Aria Greco as we have always been.*

"What a wonderful story, Sofia," Marla said, she and Julie breaking into applause. "Aria saved those two little girls."

Amazed gratitude and joy filled Sofia's heart. "It is wonderful. It certainly shines a flattering light on Aria's character."

"There's more," Clara said, "but I must swear you to secrecy before I share it."

EPILOGUE

Cabot Falls, Vermont
Present Day

The front doorbell rang, and Sofia hurried to answer. Her sisters, Gina and Rosa, were standing on the steps. "I'm so glad you both took time out of your vacations to come over." Instead of consecutive weeks, her siblings had decided to spend their time at the lake together.

"No problem." Gina smiled as she hugged Sofia. "I know you didn't want to bring the quilt over to the cottage."

"That would not be a good idea." Rosa pecked Sofia on the cheek in greeting. "It's very precious."

"It is indeed. Come on through. We're out in the four-season room." Sofia led the way to the back of the house.

The sisters exchanged greetings with Marla and Julie, and after Sofia served them iced tea and finger sandwiches, they settled down to munch and listen.

Sofia relayed the story of Aria's background as a screenwriter, her voyage on the *Titanic*, and the rescue of two orphans as the ship was sinking.

"What a great story!" Gina clapped her hands. "I'm thrilled to think someone tied to our quilt saved those poor little girls."

"Me too," Rosa said. "She showed great compassion."

"Are you going to tell them?" Julie's smile was teasing.

"What?" Rosa asked. "Is there a problem?"

Sofia smiled at her eldest sibling. "No, quite the opposite. You see, Aria helped solve a murder on the ship too."

Gina gasped. "A murder! I never heard about a murder on the *Titanic*."

"That's because everyone kept it a secret," Marla said. "The people involved were from the highest ranks of society."

"A millionaire named Edward Thurston was murdered on the ship, shot in cold blood by a valet who worked for the Astors," Sofia said. "And yes, those Astors—John Jacob Astor IV and his new bride, Madeleine."

"I've heard of them. He died . . . so tragic." Rosa shook her head.

"It was. Anyway, Aria helped solve the mystery, along with her fiancé, an assistant purser named Charles Pierce."

"Wow, the surprises keep on coming," Gina said.

"We think the Astors and the Thurston family kept it out of the press thanks to their connections," Sofia said. "And of course, after the sinking, the tragedy overshadowed everything else. Clara, the daughter of Etta Bannister, said that Edith Thurston claimed that it was her son who'd rescued the girls. I think Aria allowed her to say that to save face."

Gina nudged Rosa, sitting beside her on the sofa. "Hasn't Sofia done a great job of tracking down what happened to the women of the quilt?"

"She has," Rosa said. "In fact, I have to admit something. At first, I wasn't sure why Nonna left you the quilt, Sofia. But now I think she knew you had the brains, tenacity, and insight to solve the mysteries behind each piece of fabric."

Sofia was touched. "Thank you, Rosa. I really appreciate that."

Her journey to discover the stories behind the quilt blocks had been incredible. Each of the women from their family's history had handled difficult situations with grace, style, and intelligence, providing real inspiration to Sofia and everyone who learned about them. She herself had been transformed by learning of their lives. She smiled at Julie and Marla. "And I've had a lot of help."

"So tell them what happened to Aria," Julie prompted, bouncing in her seat. "This is good too."

"After Aria married Charles," Sofia said, "they moved to Hollywood, where Aria continued to write screenplays and Charles worked as a camera operator. They raised three children—one adopted—and lived long, healthy lives."

"I can't believe one of our relatives lived in Hollywood," Gina said. "Are any of her movies still around?"

"They are," Marla said. "We've got them on DVD."

"Let's have movie night for the whole family."

As the others discussed Gina's plan, Sofia's thoughts drifted. She should write a book, a compilation of the stories behind each of the quilt squares. Perhaps she could give presentations, accompanied by slides of the quilt pieces. This fascinating tapestry of women's courageous lives would inspire many—she just knew it.

And maybe that had been why her grandmother had bequeathed the quilt to her. On the face of it all, she had been the least likely candidate, compared to her sisters. But now she understood that Elena Baresi had seen past the obvious. Sofia knew now that she was the one with the most to gain from—and the most to give to—the secrets of the quilt.

Thank you, Nonna, she said silently. *Thank you for such a precious gift.*